AF186704

Valhalla Victims

Life after Death Metal

Impressum (Legal Disclosure)

Bibliografische Information der Deutschen Nationalbibliothek: Die Deutsche Nationalbibliothek verzeichnet diese Publikation in der Deutschen Nationalbibliografie; detaillierte bibliografische Daten sind im Internet über dnb.dnb.de abrufbar.

Copyright © 2019 Andrew Wakeford

All rights reserved. No part of this publication may be reproduced, distributed or transmitted in any form or by any means, including photocopying, recording, or other electronic or mechanical methods, without the prior permission of the author, except in the case of brief quotations embodied in critical reviews and certain other noncommercial uses permitted by copyright law. For permission requests, please contact the author at the address below.

Any references to historical events, real people, or real places are used fictitiously. Names, characters and the use of place names are products of the author's imagination.

Front cover design: Michael Hardt

Photo: Andrew Wakeford with Bernd Wegener

Andrew Wakeford

Im Roethschesfeld 4

66129 Saarbrücken

Germany

www.wakefordphotos.com

ISBN: 9783749479931

Thanks and Dedication

Grateful thanks to:

My good friend and expert drummer Bernd Wegener. The invisible hand on the cover photo is his and he was partly the inspiration for Geoff.

Our son Daniel, another drummer whose first attempts at drumming began when he was still wearing a babygrow. He gave me useful insight into a scene about which I knew little.

My old mate Michael Hardt, whose guidance and appreciation made the whole thing possible. His experience and judgement are second to none. Thanks, Mick!

Thale Goodluck, who I met in 2015 when he provided me with my first true introduction to Native American culture.

My wife Christa, who has spent much of her life tolerating my odd ideas.

Stephen Poplin, for his spiritual work and literature influence.

This book is also dedicated to an unknown set of traffic lights, as the catalyst for its inspiration. While waiting in a queue for the lights to change, the subtitle came into my head.

"I'll let you be in my dreams if I can be in yours!"

Talking World War III Blues, © Bob Dylan 1963

1.The Guys

My name is Geoff, Geoffrey Kent to be precise. At least, that was
my name before I died, but I'll get back to that later. Kent like the
county, although I was born in Sussex, my mum came from near
Tunbridge Wells and said the family always had connections to the
county of Kent. Whatever, I was never fascinated enough by a
surname to check up on it, but Mum was keen on things like roots
and heritage. Maybe because I was her only child and she was still
single when she had me. Any relationships she had after my birth
were of the short and sweet kind. Even as a 7 or 8 year old, I saw
that she was often upset at the end of another promising
relationship that never seemed to work out. It may have been the
frightening prospect of becoming a father to me that put the guys

off, and as if to prove my case, after I left home at 18, it took her less than a year to find the love of her life.

Mum was still an attractive woman in her early 40s, and had her own flower shop in Hurstpierpoint, so the love of her life didn't feel he had to support her and promptly married her. When she first came to me to tell me about her serious relationship, our roles had swapped over and it took her much longer than I expected to actually come out with the fact that she was going to marry him. I was a bit alarmed when she told me that Brian, her future husband, was going to move in with her into the flat over the shop. Okay, Brian was divorced and had a bit of a settlement to take care of but at the time I thought it was a bit opportunistic of him to move into my place, just like that. But we got on okay, he was sensible enough to be neither the father nor the good mate, and treated me with surprising respect. He seemed more sceptical about my ambition to become a photographer than my parallel plan to be a drummer in a band. Just a couple of years older than my mum, Brian still had this 60s idea that being a rock musician was a good way to earn your keep. Mum thought photography would be a more reliable source of income, but I ended up hedging my bets.

I was attending art college in Brighton when they got married. The spring of 1990, I was studying art and design, specialising in photography. Although desktop publishing was showing that the days of Letraset and 'real' copy and paste were numbered, I wasn't as interested in that as I was in making pictures by photographic means. Neither a very good draftsman nor painter, but making pictures generally was the only thing I thought worthwhile, apart from music, that is. I had two mates at college, Jay Holmes, who had been my best friend since early school days and we decided to go to the same college partly so we could continue to hang out together. His name was actually the same as mine, except spelled 'Jeffrey' so he got called Jay from his teens onwards, just to tell us apart. Jay could draw things from memory that would blow me away. Give him a pad and a pencil and he would draw anything from Brighton pier to Dürer's hare, without looking up or referring to anything outside his own mind. We also became friends at college with a guy called Mike Turner, who was a genius with electronic things. Sound, as well as anything else he set his mind to. Mike was an art student too, even though his interests seemed more technical, but he would produce radio programmes or sound installations that really stood out in their originality.

He made an installation called "Sound World" which I really loved and will never forget. He was keen on mechanics as much as electronics and combined them in a wonderful Heath Robinson way, so you could walk behind it and discover all the intricate details. Basically it was a series of sensors, set at different levels which would send out audio messages or brief musical clips, according to the height of the person who walked in. So a child, or an adult in a wheelchair, would hear a completely different version, from, say, a guy of 6 foot 2. Birdsong, snatches of pop music, different recordings of laughter, waves crashing on Brighton's beach, whales, all manner of sounds he had collected or made himself. Connected through tape decks, CD players or LPs it was impossible to hear the same version twice. Something about it was not just fun, it was funny too, although difficult to explain why. But most people seemed to come out of it smiling.

The three of us were together most evenings after college, sometimes genuinely helping each other on projects, but more often than not hanging out at some of the best pubs and clubs the Brighton and Hove area had to offer. Our music kept us together, Jay played guitar and Mike bass and keyboards so my drumming was what would have made a perfect fit, if we'd had a singing voice worthy of the name. Our voices weren't hopeless, they were just about okay for background vocals, but none of us had the vocal power or ego necessary to drive a band, so we just played covers with other musicians or jammed around. It was only a hobby and sometimes we would go for weeks without a proper gig. We had a strong connection though, which meant we didn't need to hang out together all the time. It was probably a good thing that we were all specialising in different things at college, so we saw each other as mates, rather than competitors.

2.Early Life

As a small child, it seemed to me my Mum was always busy, but living above the flower shop, it seldom felt as if she was that far away. When she was out delivering, Grandma would come and take care of the shop as well as taking care of me, which must have been a challenge when I was very young. But I only have good memories of that time, such as they are, in all their likely inaccuracies. Grandma was very concerned about bringing me up properly, so I may have had more in common with my own mother than with my peers as far as that goes.

Grandma herself had been brought up in quite a strict Methodist household, but explained to me on many occasions that she didn't go for religion at all and when she left home she rebelled against any kind of higher authority. Although she passed this on to Mum and to me, I later felt she was strict in what I thought was a kind of Methodist tradition, just without the church trimmings. She would ration things like tv (not more than 3/4 hour per evening), Dundee fruitcake (only one and a half slices at teatime), Weetabix (just two and only for breakfast), wearing shoes in the house (restricted to the entrance corridor, after that, only slippers please) and all sorts of other, seemingly random choices. I was powerless to protest about any of this until I was in my teens, and sensing that it was going to be hopeless anyway, she made much less of it from then onwards.

Widowed Grandma never remarried. I felt sure she would have done in our time, but she chose not to through a sense of duty and loyalty, never having had another real male friend according to what my Mum remembers. Her husband, John, had come back from the war with severe injuries, both physical and mental, as she would explain. As a bomb disposal expert, he had been subject to all sorts of dangerous situations. It was 'learning by doing' when he was first assigned to the job, Grandma would explain to me. Which was a very dangerous way to learn and early on he lost a number of colleagues through accidental deaths. Removing nitroglycerine was very laborious and another danger, and it was sometimes impossible not to inhale the fumes, despite protection. This gave him lasting and constant breathing problems. She never really expected him to last for very long, so that when he died in 1955 she was absurdly grateful that he had managed to hang on for that long according to what Mum told me. They had known each other from a young age, and for Grandma, it was a deliberate choice to remain loyal to him after they'd been married as soon as they could towards the end of the war.

"John made an enormous effort to stay alive. First during the war and then later with me," she would often say at teatime and wipe away a tear. This to me was in clear contradiction to the strong, resolute woman that I was used to, and I didn't ask her for more details. But it cemented a strong connection to my mother too, as we both had to manage much of life without a dad around.

Mum seemed to keep to the same rules herself, in a default kind of way. It seemed like a habit to me, but if she suspected I was trying to manipulate her by saying "Grandma said I could" - whatever it happened to be - it backfired because she knew exactly what Grandma allowed and what she didn't. Mum was loving towards me, even though she wasn't often particularly demonstrative about it. She used to tell me how guilty she felt towards me as a child, for neglecting me, even though I didn't feel at all neglected. Grandma was always there, I was never really left to my own devices. Nowadays I wonder if she felt guilty because she seldom hugged or kissed me, but the relationship we all had, if not conventional, felt fine to me. I didn't miss a dad, or a grandad for that matter.

In fact I didn't catch on for quite a while that a man was missing in our household so I pretty much grew up thinking that females were the stronger sex. As Grandpa had died in the 50s, even Mum had only fading memories of him. But he was still a major influence on my life. I used to spend hours looking through Grandma's photo albums. Pictures of him in his soldier's uniform fascinated me. But he had also been a keen amateur photographer and I spent hours poring over old prints in his carefully assembled album collection. His negatives were equally interesting and the darkroom that he had set up in their basement was still potentially in working condition and as soon as Grandma let me loose, I would later reprint his stock, thumbing first through books to work out how to dilute the developer and mix the hypo for fixing the prints. She had kept everything under wraps, so when we carefully removed them, the equipment underneath was still in pristine condition.

I loved it down in the basement, it gave me a perfect excuse to visit Grandma's place, ten minutes from the shop. It took me a long time to pluck up the courage to actually use his camera equipment, although I would often lovingly play with it. When he died, Grandpa left plenty of unexposed roll films as well as some exposed and undeveloped films too. I knew one day I would develop them, but I wanted to feel confident in my abilities first. Everything was out of date by 35 years at least, but it wasn't going to put me off trying.

At 14 I joined a local photographic club and learned some practical tricks of the trade, so that I finally took the plunge and began to develop some of the films that had been waiting for processing since the nineteen-fifties. They turned out reasonably well if a little grainy, but I'd been warned about that owing to their age. Most of the subject matter I had often come across among his archives. Birling Gap, Beachy Head, the Seven Sisters, all of which had skies in various stages of darkness. By this time I realised he had been experimenting with the yellow, orange and red filters that were in his camera bag. The red filter effect was the most dramatic, increasing the contrast between sky and clouds. I also noticed that he had used a tripod with the red filter, because of the increase in exposure time. The first shots in the series had camera shake and after that, they were pin sharp. So that was why he had written "+ 3 stops: tripod!" on the red filter case. Nice one, Grandpa, thank you! My first practical lesson in photography was being passed down through generations.

It was time to expose some of the remaining stock. Encouraged by the quality of the results so far, I thought I'd put some of the knowledge gained from each source into practice. The film stock had become quite stiff which made it somewhat difficult to load into the camera. It was a twin-lens reflex Rolleiflex and we were finally good to go. I treated it with reverence, a status that I thought it deserved. Despite its age the shutter and mechanics generally were working well. I packed the red filter, the exposure meter and the tripod and made for the bus stop, to take me to Ditchling Beacon for its first outing. All I did was shoot pictures of clouds over the Downs, and when the twelve exposures were full, made my way home again in excited anticipation.

The developing tank had space for two films, so I loaded one of the other films that was lying around undeveloped. Hanging up the still wet film, I noticed that my mother and grandmother were both featured on the old film. There was also a shot with a boy about Mum's age at the time, maybe 4 or 5 years old. I printed that one up first and brought it home to show Mum.

"Who's that Mum?" I asked her. She looked at it in a non-committal way and said she thought it was a neighbour that she used to play with.

"No, I can't remember his name."

"So he's not my Dad, then?" She just gave me a withering look, so not much point in pursuing that avenue, I realised.

....

I badgered Mum on many occasions to tell me who my father was. I had this idea that as she had had a vague connection to musicians, my dad might have been a Rolling Stone. Her connection to rock music, such as it was, came from once delivering flowers backstage at an Elton John concert when he played Brighton, but I thought she must have had an affair with Keith Richards at least.

"Or what about Brian Jones?" I asked her. "He had children all over the place!"

"He died before you were born, silly!"

She never let on and humoured my various suggestions with patience most of the time. I gave up asking when I was about 16 or 17, thinking she must have had her reasons. I even wondered whether Grandma really knew who had fathered me, as her answers appeared based more on ignorance than secrecy. But at least Grandpa had a personality that I could identify with. His image was one that I felt close to, when the void of the missing father sometimes did feel in need of some sort of fulfilment. I would have imaginary conversations with him while I sifted through the negatives. Sometimes I imagined him in my dreams, mostly in his role of safely disposing of bombs.

In our teens, Jay and I would talk quite a lot about families. He complained that his family was really boring. He had both parents and two older sisters. Susan, the oldest child, had already left home by then. I think she was more that 10 years older than Jay and they didn't have much in common, seeing each other only on occasions like Christmas and sometimes birthdays. Susan got married in her early twenties and did something in administration for the Brighton Council. Her husband, George, worked at a bank and Jay thought that was really uncool, and he would make fun of him whenever he could. I was once a witness to Jay's behaviour on a Christmas holiday, but George was able to give as good as he got. Better in fact. As I remember it, the conversation went something like this:

"George, do you find fulfilment in life by lending people money that they can't afford for things they don't need?"

I remember looking across at Susan, expecting her to look angry, yet she had an expression of satisfaction, knowing, no doubt, that George wouldn't be too bothered by this feeble attack.

"Absolutely. We project their future and see what they can afford and understand their needs only too well. As you may know, I work mainly with mortgages and I think wanting a roof over your head is a definition of necessity."

For Jay, provoking his brother-in-law was a sport, but he seldom came out on top. But it did give me a kind of insight into the complexity of family life. As for the middle sister, Jenny, even Jay had to admit she was cool. About three years his senior, she didn't treat him with contempt when he asked questions about music, if she felt he was being sincere. Jenny's interest was actually a bit of an anachronism, as at that time, folk music was about as out as you could get. She wasn't in the least bit interested in current trends in music, we thought she was obsessed with Joan Baez whose guitar picking and chord choices became Jay's first introduction to playing music himself. Indirectly, they also became my first introduction to do-it-yourself music.

Jay worked out the chords for 'The night they drove old Dixie down' with Jenny's help while I was sitting in their basement. A simple tune with an easy beat, that I started tapping in time to it on the bar they used for occasional parties. We must have been 12 or 13 at the most, but Jay had this maniacal look in his eyes and said,

"Hey, you need to learn drumming! Then we can be pop stars and go out on the road!"

"Good idea, Jeff." Jenny didn't appear to be mocking her brother at all. "If you want to tell the world something you need to get out there and do it."

I idolised Jenny in those days. I mean she was quite old, at sixteen, but I thought she was brilliant at everything she did, and I felt attracted to her despite the age difference. Her long, Joan Baez-like 60s hairstyle made her look quite romantic and the fact that she took her brother seriously was another point in her favour.

Jay himself preferred to treat it as mockery.

"Yeah, well you'd know all about that, of course!"

She left the room at that point commenting,

"Whatever."

I couldn't understand how he could treat his sister like that, but the rules of engagement simply didn't relate to my experience in the world so far. Evidently siblings talk in code much of the time, I decided. After all, she wouldn't have helped him with the chords if she didn't....well what? Love him, I supposed that meant. I was insanely jealous at the thought of being loved by Jenny, and also realised the code enabled kindness to be shared without embarrassment. A disguise for an outsider perhaps, but the participants clearly understood their rules.

....

Jay and I now had a mission, it was exciting to be a part of it. Walking around the village centre, we spotted a drum in a charity store going for so little money that even I could afford it. Turned out to be a snare drum on its own stand and they were glad to get rid of it. Little did I know that I was going to pay more for the drumsticks than for the drum, but there was no stopping us now. Jay had an acoustic guitar that Jenny no longer used, so with this minimum of equipment we set out to make a name for ourselves.

Compared to mine, Jay's family was quite posh. His father was a GP and his mother a dentist. They drove Range Rovers and other posh vehicles. I think his mum had an open top Audi for a while. They played golf. But one thing they had in common with my own roots was a love for 60s music. Their basement room (or Cavern Club as his dad called it) blasted the same kind of material through enormous speakers as my own mother played at our home. So I could sing along with Dusty Springfield, the Beatles, Buddy Holly, Elvis, etc. with the best of them. Parties over at their house were probably quite tame but they seemed wild to me at the time. A couple of pallets, covered with an old carpet made a makeshift stage and sometimes Jenny played her latest folky number to critical parental appraisal.

Sometimes, even Roger (Jay's dad) would get up and sing himself. No-one, apart from his wife had the courage to tell him how hard it was on the ears, but it was usually connected to the amount of wine consumed, so he was more or less immune to criticism and just had a good laugh. Mum came with me from time to time and she mostly enjoyed herself as well. She hardly ever drank to excess, except on one occasion I remember her removing her shoes to sing along with Sandie Shaw's 'Always something there to remind me' and taking her home somewhat tipsy afterwards, we crossed the school playing fields on the way home to our shop and I had to be careful that she didn't fall over. Hanging on to me as if she was blind drunk, though I thought it really couldn't be that bad, it was a moment I thoroughly enjoyed. Maybe she found it easier to be physically close to me in that state. We got stuck in a muddy patch while crossing the field, and she seemed to think it was hilarious to stand there in a dry patch while I retrieved he left shoe from the mud. I cherished that evening for a long time.

The worst thing about those evenings was when they would all sing along with those 60s hits, apparently unaware of how jarring it was to hear at high volume through their speakers along with their own voices through mics that Roger had set up for the purpose. It was my home from home, or family from family, you might say, and made me realise posh people weren't so very different from us.

....

But our musical careers was extremely slow in starting. We increased our repertoire somewhat and managed recognisable versions of 'Billie Jean', 'Every breath you take' and other 80s hits, but it got a bit hard to motivate each other as it was just the two of us. Once we played at the 'Cavern' in front of some of Jenny's friends and it really didn't go down well. Comments like "Don't give up your day jobs, guys!" were all we needed to hear to consider giving the whole episode up. Which we did for a while. School demanded more of our time when we began attending 6th form college and it was easier to concentrate more on art and A-levels than music for a while.

Career advice at school was hopeless, unless you were lucky enough to hear about a professional coming to talk. We both attended a talk with an advertising executive who spoke about design, marketing and copywriting, which was a lot more up our street. Very approachable, he stayed for a while afterwards talking to us informally. He spent a while explaining how photographers make a living in advertising and at 17, it helped me make a decision to consider turning my hobby into something that would become a career that I thought I'd enjoy.

We both applied to Brighton's Art College and were accepted. It was great to be able stay together. Jay was the brother I never had and as my best mate we were probably closer than most brothers. From trips through the neighbourhood on our BMX bikes or working out how to cover our favourite bands, speculating about girls from school or just hanging out together aimlessly, but holding very important discussions, we were pretty much inseparable for an impressive number of years. We were looking forward to Brighton, a really cool town compared to our village life in Hurst. The outside world was waiting to be discovered and we could hardly wait.

3.Relationships

It was end of term, our final year at college, June 1993. We had received our various hard-earned diplomas and decided to go out with a whole group after our graduation ceremony and celebrate at the King and Queen. A big place, with plenty of space for others from outside college to join us. Including Mike's younger sister, Geraldine. Oh boy, she was gorgeous. We had never met before and Mike had never made a particular secret about her but she was training to be a nurse so there weren't many opportunities to have met up, except for this one, our big final booze up before entering the real world.

My plan was to look for a proper job, although jobs in photography often would go straight to friends and contacts without being advertised, but I had already secured a six month paid internship at a good London studio beginning the following week. Looking at Geraldine temporarily drained my interest in London. It also ruined my interest in beer, for that night, at least. I just wanted to talk to her, and to my surprise, she had heard about me from Mike and was quite willing to sit apart from the others and have a private conversation with me. She had wavy chestnut hair, a mouth full of such regular teeth that a smile would stop you in your tracks and green eyes full of secrets and promise. After a number of unsuccessful relationships and pointless flirts that had left me feeling empty, Gerry was the suggestion of fullness, satisfaction, excitement.

I could hardly contain myself and this seemed to amuse her and she began teasing me no end. I thought it meant she wasn't interested and was just making fun of me at first. Then, because it was really quite loud in the pub, she leaned over and whispered in my ear that we should maybe go somewhere quieter. I say 'whispered' but it was more of a shout to make herself heard above the din, but for a shout it felt remarkably intimate and close. I agreed, so we made our way through the drunken crowd with as little fuss as possible, despite Jay's beery protest and Mike's look of concern. I saw a change in his expression take place when he noticed what was going on which made me think it might have been a nod of approval.

Outside, Gerry took my hand as if it were the most natural thing to do, and that was exactly how it felt. We turned right, somewhat aimlessly towards the Royal Pavilion, but we didn't have a proper destination in mind. Most pubs were too full and loud anyway. On reaching the pier we went down the steps on the left and onto Brighton's pebbled beach. We were talking quite a lot about plans, hers and mine, with my London internship soon to begin. Sitting on those hard stones, we looked across the water to an almost full moon reflecting on the sea and began kissing. To be honest, she instigated it, but I was keen to respond. I also felt pretty sure I was going to take it, and Gerry, quite seriously. Whether she felt the same way was hard to judge, but she certainly seemed interested that night.

We agreed to meet next day at her parents' house. I must have looked a bit alarmed about meeting them so soon, although Mike had introduced us some time ago, but that was as his friend, not her boyfriend.

"They won't be home in the afternoon, don't worry. Hey, the thought of meeting them really scares you!" she giggled. I declined to comment, but she was right, no doubt about that.

I walked her back to Mike's flat in Hove where she was spending the night. She apologised for not asking me up which I thought was sweet, and a good sign. It would have seemed a bit weird to spend the first night together in her brother's flat, so we said our goodbyes at the front door and I made my way back to the seafront. By that time it was well after midnight and I wasn't sure quite how I'd get home to Lewes, but I didn't really care. It was low tide and I walked along the beach, on the hard, damp sand that is only exposed when the tide's out. To say I had a spring in my step would be an underestimation. From the beach, I walked almost as far as the park at Stanmer when a couple about my age stopped their car and asked if I wanted a lift. I was happy to do so but in my dreamy state I'd have made it home on foot too, if I'd had to. I slept in this same state, and although I couldn't remember any specific dreams next morning, I had the feeling that a new, exciting chapter of my life was unfolding.

On Saturday afternoon I made my way to their address in Moulsecoomb. Gerry opened the door in a green teeshirt and jeans. I'd been pondering about whether or not we would carry on where we had left off, but I needn't have worried. Grabbing me by the arm, she dragged me inside, then closing the front door, she pushed me up against it and gave me a big hungry kiss, pushing her hands under my shirt. With her mouth close to my ear, she said,

"Good to see you Geoff. I've been missing you!" as she playfully bit on an earlobe. I think I can safely claim that my heart had never beaten so fast up to that point in my life, but I still tried to put up a bit of a protest.

"Hey, let me get in first!"

But she wasn't having any of it and dragged me upstairs to her room. I had never known a girl quite like this before. She was obviously in control and enjoying it. I mean, I've always gone for strong women, but Gerry was in another league entirely. With her hands under my shirt again she dragged it over my head, while I noticed with a slight sense of shock that she had a Wham! poster on the wall. The sense of shock left me when I saw a Nirvana poster next to the window, but these distractions probably only took a couple of milliseconds to process. Next to come was my belt and jeans and while she let me remove her teeshirt, she didn't want to bother with fumbling, so she removed her bra and her own jeans herself so that we were standing there in our underwear looking at each other. Gerry seemed to be on the verge of laughter a lot of the time and I found it quite a turn-on. Next thing we were on her bed without any clothes on at all, and I assumed we would soon be sleeping with each other. But she slowed me down and looked at me from a crouched position on the bed. Her fingers explored my head and my face as if trying to memorise it all as she pushed a thumb between my lips. I bit on it gently and she seemed to think it was a hilarious thing to do and withdrew it with an expression of over-the-top pretend-pain.

"Oh Geoff, why haven't we met before?"

"I don't know," I replied, "maybe Mike was hiding you on purpose?"

"Or he was waiting for a good moment!" she giggled again.

"Well this is certainly a good one," I suggested, looking into her eyes and drawing her closer. We kissed like we had kissed on Friday night and I felt the same urgency and passion, but Gerry wasn't going to lose control of the situation. She played with my mood and my desire and drove me nuts, in a good way, if there is such a thing. Hugging and caressing each other for quite a time, I knew I'd never ever known this intimacy before and I wanted to hold onto it for ever.

When we finally slept together, she was on top, looking at me with the same mesmerising look that she'd had before. I wanted to crawl inside those green eyes of hers - I felt hypnotised by her looks. I climaxed pretty quickly, but I saw more amusement that she had got me so aroused than disappointment at it being over so soon. It was a warm afternoon and we slept half an hour or so in afterglow, when my paranoia about her parents returned.

"When do you expect them back?" I asked her anxiously.

"About 5-ish," Gerry glanced casually at her alarm clock. It was ten to five and we both jumped when we realised how the time had flown.

We hurried ourselves back into our clothes and ran down the stairs, taking the backdoor to leave via the garden and the lane behind it.

Once outside we soon felt safe and Gerry explained that her parents were quite broad-minded and wouldn't have been too shocked if they'd found us together.

"Even so, I'm glad they didn't find us in flagranti!" Gerry laughed at the idea and put her arm round my waist and squeezed me.

"I'm glad we found each other though, aren't you?"

She was looking at me with a serious expression now, really wanting to know.

"You bet, Gerry, you bet!"

She bit my earlobe again and laughed a throaty laugh that I hadn't heard before. Then letting go of me, she rushed across the main road to the traffic island while there was an opportunity to do so, and waved at me as if I'd been a long way off. I couldn't help laughing at this extraordinary girl, who was so childlike in some ways and grown-up in others. I caught up with her in the playing fields opposite where she was determined to keep amusing herself with various antics. In some ways I found it hard to make the connection to Mike, they didn't seem to have much in common, apart from this playfulness they shared. I'd never had a sibling relationship to compare it to, but it seemed quite different from Jay and his sisters. I had only known strong women. Gerry was strong in a different way, but then again, she was strong too.

We walked into town together, a fair distance that we hardly noticed. She pointed out the hospital where she was training to be a nurse was located, and we talked vaguely about plans. It was early days, really early days to be making plans, so we kept the conversation as casual as we could. Brighton being Brighton, we just walked around aimlessly and still enjoyed wasting time without a particular goal in mind. An occasional coffee here, a beer there and a look at secondhand books on display in the Lanes was about the sum total of our late afternoon. We finished up with another visit to the beach, where we watched kids playing with the sand at low tide. We often held each other tight, and along with the kissing and caressing, I felt an urgency in this new relationship.

As it was early summer it didn't get dark till late, and we made our way finally across to the bus stop and went upstairs while there was still some daylight left. She got out at Moulescoomb, insisting I wasn't to take her home, much as I wanted to. Sadly, I knew her grandparents were coming next day, so we decided not to meet up.

I left on Sunday evening for London, wanting to avoid the next morning's commuter train. Got to Wimbledon where I was staying with another college buddy, to start my new life. Rob Clarkson had moved to Wimbledon to work as a trainee art director in an up and coming design agency, Spicer and Friends. He was into graphic design and my photography wasn't competition for his line of work at all, so we got on well together. He had also been responsible for getting me the internship. The studio frequently worked with Spicers and he had asked - just like that - and they had agreed, just like that. The flat belonged to a family member of Rob's, which was a twist of luck that actually made my whole venture in London affordable.

I found I was working quite hard from the word go, but absorbed though I was by the studio comings and goings during the day, my focus was mostly on seeing Gerry again. She waited patiently for me to get home each Friday, but I connected the two points of my life by photographing her every weekend. She loved to flirt with the camera and it made my day to watch her act out her erotic appeal with such abandon. Developing and printing the black and white images at the studio during the following week then partly made up for the loneliness I felt in London. Rob worked long hours, and after a while I would do the same so we might see each other for a quick coffee in the morning, if that. Sometimes work demanded that I did overtime, but if not, I would lovingly print out a couple of the best shots from the weekend and then make my way back to Wimbledon by tube, keeping the prints safe in a package under my arm. I didn't usually feel happy about looking at the prints on the underground, so I rewarded myself with a proper look when I got back to the flat. Gerry sustained me, she was my reason for working and my motivation to return to Sussex at the weekend. This is how we carried on for a couple of months, and it seemed to me like a satisfactory arrangement, given that Gerry was tired during the week and went to bed early. An exchange student was renting my flat near Lewes for the working week, but I was keen to return to it and reclaim it as my own at weekends.

I had taken a series of shots of her up at the Devil's Dyke. When we got there, it had just stopped raining and the sun was out, although it seemed to be going in and coming out all the time. It was reasonably warm, but very windy. I used a yellow filter to enhance the dramatic skies while Gerry undid her blouse, exposing her thin teeshirt and upper body to the elements. The combination of movement of the material she was wearing, the force of the wind and the slow shutter speed I had chosen, produced a lot of blur movement in her blouse and she was looking just away from the camera into the distance, across the Sussex Downs, in the shot I picked as my favourite. It was great to have something to look forward to during my next week at work, and I chose one particular shot without hesitation on Monday evening back in London. Tuesday and Wednesday were reserved for printing, and although most people knew at the studio what I was up to, they weren't particularly inquisitive, except for Jane, our studio angel.

Jane's proper job was bookkeeping, but she became so good at general organising, casting and styling, that she was given more responsibilities than her job description suggested. I found her in the darkroom, bent over the waste bin, when I went in there to retrieve a light stand that we had been using in there and I had forgotten about.

"Anything I can do to help, Jane?" I asked her.

She had two prints that I had discarded in her hands. They were a bit stuck to each other, and I remember being disappointed that both were too light and I'd thrown them away.

"Are these yours, Geoff?" she asked me, while peeling the still slightly moist surfaces apart.

"Yes, why? I thought I was allowed to use the darkroom and equipment?" I said a bit defensively.

Jane gave me a look that said it all - that it was a stupid and unnecessary question.

"It's a very good shot. Do you have a decent print you can lend me for a bit?"

"Um, yes, I suppose so."

She laughed and told me I needed to be more enthusiastic, if I was ever going to make a go of photography.

"No, that's fine. What do you want to do with it?"

"Did you meet Terry last week? Terry Bride. He is an art director who came round last week after seeing Maurice's portfolio. He's interested in working with us as he likes Maurice's style and he mentioned something about an up and coming campaign, where this might be suitable."

"Okay," I replied. "I'll bring my best print tomorrow."

"You do that, thanks, Geoff." Jane left the darkroom after debating with herself what she should do with the discarded prints, but decided the bin probably was the best place for them. She obviously trusted me, too.

Maurice Bailey was one of the freelancers who would come and go in the studio. Sharing his last name with David Bailey, one of Britain's most renowned photographers, didn't do his career any harm. I always liked to assist Maurice, he had an offhand sort of charm, which I thought clients interpreted as confidence, but he confessed to me fairly early on in our acquaintance that it was all bluff.

"To begin with I don't really know what the hell I'm doing. If the client gives me a layout and you guys set up the lights and I do a couple of polaroids, that's when I think we might be creating a reasonable image. I mean people pay a lot of money for us, so we have to give them the impression that we know what we are up to."

I didn't believe a word of it. He was less than ten years older than I was but I thought he had a magic touch for getting these scenes of artificial optimism to look natural and authentic. He would always stop for a tea or coffee break if we were working too hard without getting close to a great result. After coffee, he was more open for new ideas, or had some of his own and we honed in on the problem with renewed energy. He was a good teacher, although I'm sure he didn't see himself in that role.

....

Next day I brought in my best print of Gerry. Jane held it at arm's length and decided, yes, she'd like to show it to Maurice. We soon heard a cab drawing up outside the studio, and we both assumed it was Maurice arriving. While he paid the taxi, she considered the best strategy knowing he'd be in the office soon.

"Let's just leave it on the desk, without making a big deal out of it. Are you okay with that, Geoff?"

"Sure," I said, not quite sure where this was going.

Maurice waltzed into the office and we wished him a good morning without any great ceremony. But his eye was caught by my print and he didn't waste any time to have a good look at it.

"Wow, who did this Isadora Duncan reshoot?" I vaguely knew the image he was referring to, although I knew I couldn't seriously be compared to its masterful photographer, Edward Steichen.

Jane evidently didn't want him to find out too quickly, and she gave me a look that I should keep mum.

"Do you like it Maurice? I was thinking of showing it to Terry this week."

"Terry Bride? Do you mean for his deodorant campaign? That's not a bad plan. He said he was running out of ideas, so it could be a great move. But who took it, who is the lovely girl?" At that point, Jane couldn't contain herself, and pointed to me.

"Geoff did it at the weekend, and that's his girlfriend, Geraldine." Photographers are generally suspicious of up and coming competition, fearing their own demise, but Maurice had a completely different idea.

"He could sell the idea as a layout and we could reshoot in colour." Then turning to me, he asked,

"Or did you shoot in colour as well, Geoff?" I swallowed my disappointment, but as I hadn't shot in colour, I knew he was right.

Terry turned up on Friday afternoon and went quite overboard with delight.

"This is just what we need. It's great! I wonder if we could handcolour it?" He didn't seem to be serious, but using it as a layout photo to show the client what the idea was, already seemed a pretty cool thumbs-up for my weekend enjoyment. It would also be paid extra! I couldn't wait to get back to Brighton to tell Gerry the good news.

But Gerry didn't give me the chance to do so. Meeting me at the station that evening, she welcomed me with a peck on the cheek and an obviously changed mood.

"Geoff, I'm so sorry but it's over between us. I'm seeing someone else and it wouldn't be fair on him to meet up with you like this anymore. Oh yes, and I'm pregnant and he's very happy about it. We are going to stay together."

I was so shocked by all of this I must have looked like a complete head case, trying to absorb what the love of my life had just told me. My first thought when I finally managed to form one, was that surely I was the father if there was a baby on its way. She had always said she had everything under control and when we didn't use contraception, it was because it was a safe time of the month, as she put it. My next thought was about the hours I'd spent in the darkroom, which wouldn't have made any sense to her. I was then aware of anger rising, and although I didn't feel anything like violence towards her, but I could have broken something if they'd been a convenient object nearby.

"I bet he's a bloody doctor!"

"No, he isn't! At least not yet."

It was so classic, I felt like laughing bitterly in Gerry's face. But I found I couldn't look at her anymore. Gerry had made me feel complete and now I felt like an empty shell. I wished her all the best as sincerely as I could and turned around to look for a distraction.

Lacking the will to get drunk, in fact lacking the will to do anything, my motivation was left stranding in Brighton station. I felt utterly, completely, miserable. How could she reject me without so much as an apology worth the name? Walking down Queen's Road, I was in a cloud of separation from the rest of the world. Everything in front of me or to my side looked fuzzy and I was isolated within my own head, trying to make sense of my new situation. I vaguely thought of the "whores on 7th Avenue" where Paul Simon had taken some comfort, but the girls that I saw didn't seem to be plying any sort of trade and were ignoring me anyway. I felt invisible, so when I got to the sea-front I turned left towards the pier. Walking down the few steps leading to the banjo groyne, I felt that all the noises people and traffic around me were making came from a distant place to which I had no access. Getting to the end of the concrete breakwater, I looked out into the sea, waves breaking against this massive support, and it felt vaguely comforting. For the first few moments, I was attracted to the idea of jumping in and moving out of this weird unfocused zone. The cold and potential lack of comfort held me back though, in spite of everything I didn't feel suicidal. Thoroughly depressed, yes, but not suicidal. Walking on the pebbled beach , I noticed the extreme hardness of the stones, in sharp contrast to my usually positive experience of the beach. It was reflecting a feeling of hardness and hostility that I hadn't felt before. I had no idea what to do with myself. I hadn't been seeing the guys very much since I had started going out with Gerry and they had their own new lives to live and careers to follow too. We all had keys to the rehearsal room where Mike worked and I started out with the vague intention of walking there. I still couldn't see the world around me as a place that I was currently a part of. I wasn't even thinking about Gerry so much as how weird it was to be an observer, but not a participant within this changed world. I was half hoping that a familiar face would recognise me and bring me back to reality. In this oddly dreamlike state, I finally caught a bus and made it back to my flat in Lewes.

....

Waking up on that Saturday morning, I felt that my usual energy had disappeared without trace. Gerry was gone, the one who had been sustaining me every recent weekend. I was feeling so low, that I couldn't make the effort to get up until it started to get dark that evening. I needed a bite to eat, too, but I was so lacking in the will to do anything that I didn't even feel properly hungry. I wondered about calling Gerry, but dismissed it. The train had left the station, no other interpretation was possible. I tried to picture her new boyfriend and went through any number of faces I could conjure up, but apart from a kind of general jealousy, I didn't feel anything matched. It made the rage that I had initially felt a kind of waste with nothing for it to focus on. Only emptiness replacing the fullness that I had been getting used to in recent weeks. Emptiness and complete loss of energy.

Sunday came and went without any change in my mood. But at least I still had the self-discipline to return to London. Back at the photo studio the Monday after the fateful weekend on my own, Jane asked if I had asked Gerry if she would agree to pose for a deodorant shoot. I explained we were now talking about my ex and I had no intention of asking her. Jane, bless her, looked quite shocked.

"Oh Geoff, I'm so sorry to hear that."

While it was something Jane had to accept, it also put her under a lot of pressure to find a replacement but I think she genuinely was more sorry for me to begin with. Terry had liked the shot and the model, it turned out. By the time Jane had chosen three favourites from her well-trusted model agencies, we were getting close to the end of November, not really a suitable time of year for an outside shoot. Terry and Maurice agreed that one of the girls, Maggie, would be the best replacement and although she was blonde, I had to agree she had a similar look, so we prepared a shoot at the same location, with the intention of recreating the atmosphere of early autumn, instead of the unavoidable Christmas mood that was already evident almost everywhere. We looked like a mini Hollywood production, with a location van, make-up artist Jessie, two electric generators, a powerful ventilator, several studio flash packs and flash heads, Maggie, Maurice, Terry, Jane, Ken, who was soon to replace me as the main assistant, and myself. Jane was responsible for the styling and I was responsible for the Sussex weather.

"Maurice, you do know we'll be nearly on the south coast, where "changeable" is the closest you'll get to a forecast?" I argued with Maurice to no avail in the days beforehand.

"There is no point in postponing it now Geoff, we will lose the job if we can't deliver soon. You work your magic with the lighting and I'm sure it'll be fine," he replied, grinning.

"But why don't we go the South of France, instead of the South of England?"

"Because wherever you look in France there's nowhere that looks quite like the Weald, and the landscape is a good part of what makes this visual concept work. It would also cost at least twice as much. And as far as the weather goes, changeable means at least we have a good chance of some sunshine and not continuous rain!"

I was thinking about the number of hours of daylight, let alone sunshine that we could expect that time of year, and I knew it was going to be hard to get it right. But I had to admire his optimism, it was like an indirect reason for his success, as he could deal it out like a pack of cards, so everyone felt we were in with a fighting chance.

The day came and I felt sorry for Maggie. Terry and Maurice were trying to keep as close as possible to the layout, but although we had a fair breeze, it was coming in from the sea, rather than towards the coast as it was on my shot. So the poor girl had to put up with a breeze from behind and a strong wind from the large ventilator in front of her. We all wore jackets, and she had a coat on until we started shooting, when the blouse was meant to flutter in the wind and she was supposed to look as if she was enjoying a late summer's day. She did very well, although I saw her shivering every time we took a short break she gladly warmed her hands on a mug of coffee. It turned into one of those crisp, cold and sunny afternoons in the end and by combining the sun and flash with an underexposed background and dappled sunlight on the Weald, Maurice topped my result for drama in the background. He was good, I had to appreciate that, but it made me smile to think how my picture had just been Gerry, my camera, tripod and me, without so much as a reflector in sight. But this was in colour and I could already see how good it would look in magazines, probably as a whole page. Photographic productions gave me solace, I loved the tension and excitement before getting something just right. Maurice had asked me about the equipment I had used (the Rolleiflex 3.5F that I had inherited from the grandfather I had never met), matching focal length and my shooting position, which was about chest high, adapting things while he was working only if they would really enhance the image. There was no way he could use the same exposure and he had to be very inventive while lighting it. But otherwise he pretty much copied my original image.

It was a Friday and there was just a bit of light left by the time we had finished. I gave Ken instructions as to what to do with the equipment and films and otherwise said my goodbyes to the team. All were in agreement that it would be unnecessary for me to go back to London with them. Jane, Jessie and Maggie gave me a hug, which brought home to me how I missed having a woman in my arms and my life, and I made my way to the station in a slightly more buoyant mood than usual, when they dropped me off on their way to the M23 to take them back to London.

Back home in Lewes, I was finding it impossible to maintain this better mood. Memories of Gerry were coming thick and fast, I was brought closer to her memory than I had realised while we were doing the shoot. I could look at the original shot dispassionately while we were working, but now, even without the print in my hands, the memory of that afternoon with Gerry was being relived over and over in my brain. I went to the local chippie for some fish and chips as we as a team had only had time for a quick sandwich break. I ate at the counter with a view looking out onto the still busy street, testing my own feelings for any changes or improvement. Maybe there had been a slight improvement, I thought I'd find out next morning.

Was it actually dark outside, I thought on waking up? Still dark, dark again, a storm-brewing darkness, or my mood playing tricks on me? It turned out to be still dark, I had woken up at 4 am and felt quite restless. Made myself a cup of tea, then went back to bed and I must have fallen asleep again as next time I looked out of the window it was almost dark. I had slept through the daylight hours, and had no reason even then to get up and do something. I put some music on, a tape that I had mixed, but then 'When a man loves a woman' came on, I had to turn it off. Maybe Percy Sledge had gone through something similar, but it was too much to listen to in my current state of mind. That, basically, is how I survived until Christmas. I even stayed in London one weekend, not that that was any kind of improvement. I was living in a permanent state of the blues, eating out from time to time to stay alive, listlessly doing the basics that needed my attention, but otherwise completely lacking in motivation and feeling thoroughly depressed. But at least I still had enough energy to get up and go to work. Sometimes I would get so absorbed in what we were up to, that I'd notice I hadn't thought about Gerry the whole day. It was a pity that drumming didn't have the same appeal. Photography was the therapy that I desperately needed to keep going.

Jane was sympathetic and always asked how I was doing, but she had the good sense not to pursue the case if my answer was a mere grunt. Maurice was over the moon with the pictures we had done in Sussex, as was Terry, the art director. He wanted to make a series out of the first shoot and Maurice was very pleased to be considered their regular photographer. He even said once,

"It's all thanks to you, Geoff!" slapping me on the back. Yes, it was pleasant to hear that, but also difficult to drum up any enthusiasm for anything. Everyone at the studio knew I was leaving after Christmas, and Jane had warned me that the camaraderie in the ad business shouldn't be mistaken for friendship.

"There's this great feeling that you are creating something together and it gets everyone high, to a certain extent, and we fall into each other's arms when something works out really well. Or maybe, fall into bed with each other, but it's very superficial and when people move on and promise to stay in touch, it's often the last time you'll ever see them. I've seen it so often."

Jane was still in her 20s, but she had worked in several places before landing with us and was probably in a good position to judge. She was great to have around and I was glad for her attention and understanding. I wasn't very good at communicating my emotional hardship, and I think she understood that it was just too hard for me to talk to her about it. Before the shoot in Brighton, I had told her about Gerry's pregnancy and my possible status of having fathered a child.

"Women generally know, Geoff. It's unlikely that she would think you were the father and just tell you it was her new lover. Even if it would create a mess, but most girls I know would think of father's rights and living with a secret isn't a great alternative. Particularly the fear of it coming out later."

I'd had no particular wish to father a child, it's true, I was way too young for that sort of thing, but I had felt a resentment that went beyond her sleeping with another guy during the week and me at weekends. But what did I know? If I had become a father it would have meant a lot of changes too, whether or not I was still in a relationship with the mother. It wasn't just the sex, which had been wonderful and exciting, it was also the first time I really cared about someone. Previous relationships had been on a kind of fuzzy agreement basis, the unspoken assumption being - 'You do know this is a one night stand, right?' And I was just as guilty of thinking that as my previous partners had been.

Life goes on. It was difficult to tolerate, but my expectation of having a miserable life in front of me wasn't a permanent thing. I felt it with Christmas fast approaching and didn't have any proper career plans for the next year, but deep down I was hoping at some point there'd be damage limitation.

....

Christmas was at Mum's and Brian kept asking me all sorts of questions, while Mum kept quiet, which made me feel a little uncomfortable. She asked about Mike and Jay and when I said I hadn't seen them for a few weeks, she went silent. So while Brian would ask me questions about drumming and photography, she looked out of the window, mainly, I thought, to avoid looking at me. Boxing Day meant meeting Brian's kids, which I wasn't keen on doing, but I turned up anyway and listened while they told me about their various successes. Both girls were somewhat younger than me, you'd think I might be interested in communicating but the best I could summon was keeping to the decent side of talking without being rude. I'm sure Mum knew I'd been through some hard times, but it was as if she couldn't decide on a strategy to confront me. I was running out of ideas too, but felt that being on my own on New Year's Eve might be a plan.

I'd received a Christmas card from Jay and Mike, so they apparently hadn't given up on me entirely. I did wonder why they had both signed the same card. Some kind of signal, no doubt, but it was beyond my understanding. I spent the weird days between Christmas and New Year watching TV and listening to some music, at least. I didn't want to be stubborn, but I was finding it way too hard to shrug off what had happened and get on with life.

So, New Year's Eve came and armed with George Orwell's 1984 (I thought that was bound to cheer me up) I went to a pub I'd never been to before, about a ten minute walk from my flat. The faux fireplace was on and I grabbed myself an armchair next to it in the secluded corner and, leaving my book on the chair, I went to the bar and grabbed my first pint of Sussex bitter. God, the music was weird! I know we have a kind of Scottish tradition on New Year's Eve, but this was bagpipes and really mournful. Some people were dancing in a vaguely Scottish way and it turned out it was someone's birthday. Someone from Scotland, no less. Fancy being born on the last day of the year, I thought to myself. Realising then that that was probably one of the first independent thoughts I'd had in quite a few weeks, I took a large gulp of my beer and got back to Winston Smith and the shit he was going through, poor sod. As I put the pint glass on the roughly hewn oak beam above the fireplace, the thought went through my mind that it was just another attempt to make the place look cosy and authentic. I decided I was going to have to be fairly quick if I wanted to make sure I'd have access to drink. The place was filling up and it was becoming harder to get to the bar. Not sure what came over me as spirits really don't agree with me but I ordered two double whiskies with my next beer, to be sure I'd have enough alcohol if the route to the bar became too much of a challenge.

Presumably, I hadn't exactly been drinking the place dry, but the whisky sent me to sleep despite the music and general noise level. I've since been told that while the place was emptying towards midnight and everyone was out on the High Street, my mouth was open and I was snoring like some old geezer. I hope I wasn't dribbling. But apparently I jumped in my sleep from time to time and I do recall snippets of extremely weird dreams. Parts of reality were mixing in with dream sequences - it was quite psychedelic. The next thing I remember was struggling to get myself into a car. Someone was helping me and I was convinced it was Mike, except it didn't smell like Mike, who used to smoke in those days. It smelled special, in a way I couldn't describe. Then the taxi driver (that's who I thought it was, anyway) came back around the other side, got in and started the car. His voice was feminine, no - it was a woman, I decided after a while. I tried to repeat my address but couldn't get my tongue round it. She said not to worry, so I didn't and went back to sleep. Arriving at a destination, she dragged me inside somewhere, first waking me up gently, or so she said later, but I was suddenly panicking that I didn't know where the hell I was.

"Don't worry, this is my place, you can spend the night on my couch."

Such a kind thing to say but to me it was just puzzling. But I still didn't really know what was happening and drifted off into another round of psychedelic dreamy sleep. Waking up before dawn, I was very confused as to where I was, who I was with and why. I also need a loo, both ends of me claiming their needs at once and I had no idea where it was. I burst through the most likely looking door and I was in luck, it was indeed the bathroom. Kneeling down over the toilet bowl I threw up first, then wiped my mouth with toilet paper, got up, turned around and satisfied the other, only slightly less urgent need. Feeling relieved at least, I risked a glance in the mirror. God, I was a mess. I heard a gentle knock at the door. Panic came over me. I didn't even know where I was or whose place this was.

"Just a moment, I need a minute." I was also feeling a cold sweat and I thought dizziness was creeping over me too. Mustn't let that happen.

"Okay, no problem. This is Sally. Just let me know if you need anything. I'll make a cup of coffee or tea if you like."

"Wow, yeah. Tea would be great. As would coffee. Whatever, I still need a couple of minutes though."

"No problem, the kitchen is to your right. I've turned the lights on in the corridor."

Deciding the least I could do would be to have a shower and tidy myself up a bit, I think I had never found myself in a more awkward situation. At least the dizziness was fading and a cold shower to begin with was probably a good idea. I was looking for a towel, when I heard her voice again.

"I have some guest bath towels on top of the washing machine. The first of the two shelves."

Well Sally sounded quite young and she had been very kind, but I didn't even know where I was, and wouldn't recognise her anywhere. Still, I imagined we were alone, so there wasn't much chance of mistaking her. After the shower I looked slightly better in the mirror and drying myself off, I put on the clothes that I came in. Looking for traces of the previous night, it was quite a relief to see I was fairly clean.

"Hello," Sally said cheerfully. "Are you feeling better?"

"Yes, I think so," I mumbled somewhat sheepishly. I had just spent the night at this girl's flat and I didn't even know who she was and what made her help me. I had vague memories of dreadful music and some singing, so I did feel a certain amount of relief that my memory hadn't completely failed me. It was still dark outside, but it didn't register that it might still be the middle of the night. Something felt more like early morning.

Taking a seat at her kitchen table I gratefully grabbed the steaming mug of tea she was holding for me and sat down. I could tell Sally was doing her best to help me relax. I wanted to introduce myself, but it felt weird in the situation. Sally held out her hand in a strangely formal attempt at introduction instead.

"Pleased to meet you, Mr Kent."

She smiled while I struggled for words.

"I saw the name G. Kent inside '1984'" she explained, "so I assumed you had written your own name on the inside cover."

I was still feeling awkward, but I had to admit this Sally was doing a good job to remove any awkwardness. She was also lovely to look at. She reminded me of Snow White, with dark hair, blue eyes and quite pale skin. Struggling to say something appropriate, I saw her look a little embarrassed for a moment, noticing that I was looking at her a little too long. But it was only fleeting, she was evidently made of stronger stuff.

"Happy New Year, Sally. It's very nice of you to take care of me, my name is Geoff, by the way. Where am I actually? What were you doing in the pub? I presume that's where you found me? Was I really awful last night?"

Sally laughed at my various questions and said I should drink my tea - it would do me good and we could talk soon. Excusing herself, she went first to the bathroom and then her bedroom and when she came back I felt my head clearing and my stomach was settling, too. I had looked out of the window hoping for a clue as to my whereabouts, but it was still dark outside and it could have been anywhere, although it didn't look much like Lewes. Just a couple of lampposts and parked cars. I saw a few detached houses opposite and a dog owner taking his dog for a morning walk. So it wasn't perhaps as early as it felt to me, but it was probably more countrified than I was used to.

Coming up behind me, Sally was apparently reading my thoughts,

"It's just off the A26 near Uckfield."

"Okay", I replied, realising right away that I sounded alarmed. Smiling again, Sally began to explain patiently,

"It's very convenient for me. Halfway between my Uncle's pub in Lewes and East Grinstead where I work. I only work at the pub at weekends, including Fridays, that is."

"Which is where you must have found me, I suppose?" the sheepishness returning to me but I had to fill the gaps.

"That's right. I spied you almost as soon as I came in. Someone on his own on New Year's Eve reading Orwell's '1984' is a bit unusual. I don't often work behind the bar itself, mostly I help make the pub food, do the washing up and clearing up, but I kept an eye in your direction whenever I could. I thought the evening wasn't going to end well for you, so I was relieved when you dropped off."

"I wasn't snoring was I?" I asked and Sally broke into a fit of giggles so that kind of answered my question.

We chatted for a while as I listened to the description of her job, which involved teaching handicapped children.

"When I came in and saw you hunched over a book, I thought you'd be in need of some help later."

I could have ended up in the gutter, could have been robbed, might not have found my way home at all, who knows? Mike and Jay wouldn't have found me last night, that's for sure. If they were giving up on me it was hardly surprising. I began to think to myself, well, it's a new year, maybe it's time for some resolutions that I can realistically keep to. Lost in thought as I was, Sally appeared at my side with a refill of tea and startled me a bit with her sudden appearance. I hadn't noticed she had left the table.

"Sorry, sorry - I didn't mean to jump. Bit lost in thought as it happens."

"That's okay," Sally said. "It's only natural." What was it that made her so kind towards me?

'The goodness of her heart,' was the only explanation I could come up with. It was Grandma's explanation for everything that seemed positive for no particular reason. Making me think about my grandmother was sad. She had died only a few years previously, and she had often been my replacement Mum.

....

Grandma had been so healthy and full of energy for her age. She was in her early 80s when she died, but the last two years or so had been hard. Hard for me and hard for my Mum. Grandma had always been bright and had an excellent memory and would often keep me on my toes with questions about school, or homework, much more than her daughter would. So it was a shock to us both when she developed dementia in her late 70s. After a few months it was obvious she would be unable to look after herself and she moved in with Mum and Brian, occupying a small room that Mum had been using for laundry and storage. Grandma didn't seem to mind, but she started treating her daughter like a stranger and she was often more civil to Brian than to Mum.

I could tell that it was a strain on their relationship too, but there wasn't much I could do about it. I was concentrating on my studies in any case and only visited them occasionally as my weekends were just as busy as my weekdays, Brighton being an interesting place to hang out even if there weren't any particular events happening.

But when I did go, I found it hard to take. Grandma didn't recognise me anymore! She didn't recognise Mum either, but I wasn't confronted with it as often, so it was a shock when I finally experienced it for the first time. Mum had told me on the phone that Grandma wasn't recognising her quite early on, this being partly the reasoning behind her moving in. But I was confident she would still know who I was, I mean wasn't I 'the apple of her eye' as she would frequently say? But no, she looked at me as if trying to make a connection, but gave up after nothing came to mind. I talked to Mum about it and witnessed Grandma's behaviour to Mum, treating her almost like a servant. Mum thought it was something she had to accept early on and showed a lot of strength in this new role.

"She was always good to me. Very supportive and loved you to bits as well. It's okay how it is now. I can give something back to her at last."

"Fair enough, Mum, but I hope she doesn't wear you out."

"I'll be fine, after all I have a man about the house now," she said with a mischievous grin.

Grandma had been living with them just over a year when she had fell down the narrow flight of stairs which led from the side entrance of the shop to the flat above. She wasn't supposed to use the stairs at all, but presumably forgot as she took her wastepaper basket downstairs and slid down the final seven or eight steps, giving her back a nasty ride. Brian was at home and heard her shout. He found her in a sorry state, crying in pain, which was apparently coming from her back and hip. He called an ambulance and she was taken to hospital where she remained until she died only 10 days later, not responding to medication for pneumonia that she had also picked up.

Mum and I were there when she died. Mum went every day and I was there twice in the ten days. She still didn't recognise us, but we were now well beyond expecting her to. She seemed in constant pain and her body would arch from time to time, which seemed to put a strain on her back and cause her further pain. It was even painful to watch and the staff said that there wasn't much they could do about it.

Then there was a moment when we both thought there was a chance of a full recovery.

She opened her eyes, looking first at me and then my Mother.

"Geoffrey," she said, as clearly as she had ever spoken. "Darling," she turned her head to Mum.

"I need to tell you two something." We looked at her in sheer amazement, both waiting with bated breath for her words. She even smiled and looked from one of us to the other, each of us standing on the same side of the bed.

"I need to tell you, because it's quite important." She had our full attention now.

"It's all going to be fine in the end." And with that she closed her eyes, the smile still on her lips. Mum and I didn't know what to make of it, we looked at her and we looked at each other, trying to make sense of what we were watching. She took one deep breath and then her breathing became quite regular, almost mechanical. After a few moments, she took one more very deep breath and was gone. We didn't need to ask anyone, it was so obvious that she had left her mortal coil. We just stood there for a while, holding hands, I noticed. Then we hugged each other and Mum and I had a really good sob, crying on each other's shoulders until we ran out of tears.

Dabbing her eyes with a tissue, Mum looked at me and said,

"Wow, that was something. That was quite something." Her tears were a mixture of sadness and joy, I don't think I had ever seen her like that before.

"Yes it was, Mum. It really was."

....

A lightweight but sudden movement woke me from my reverie, as a young kitten jumped onto my lap.

"I see you have a cat, Sally!" I called out to her in the general direction of the bedroom, where I assumed she had gone.

"Oh, you have met George!" She came out of the bathroom with a towel wrapped around her head, drying her hair.

"He's not mine, he belongs to the neighbour from next door. But he seems to have taken a shine to me and my flat. Sometimes he spends the night here and comes and goes as if the whole place were his. I usually have the window open a tiny bit, and as he's still such a small cat, it's wide enough for him to squeeze in and out. He's very affectionate."

I'd noticed that already. In fact, the volume of his purring was much louder than I would have expected from such a small bundle. His paws were pushing on my thighs and as his claws were out, he made me gasp at the minor, but unexpected pain.

"You mustn't let him do that or he'll never learn," Sally explained, coming to my rescue. "Every time his claws come out, you have to put him on the floor. And none too gently, so that he really gets the message!" She plonked him on the floor and gave his tail a slight slap, to emphasise the point.

George looked at Sally so endearingly that I had to laugh.

"I think he's trying his best to get the message."

"Yes, it's a shame we don't speak the same language so we can get though to him intellectually, so to speak."

The idea of having intellectual communication with a six month old tom cat struck us as so hilarious, that we both began laughing uncontrollably. The volume of our laughter must have scared the poor creature and he jumped onto the window sill, squeezing his tiny body through the gap as he disappeared in an instant. This made us laugh even more and we were left facing each other, still finding it hard to stop when I felt the urge to embrace her. Maybe Sally felt it too, but we both let it go. We returned to more mundane behaviour. Sally went back to the bathroom where I soon heard her hairdryer blowing, and I went back to sipping my second mug of tea.

"Happy New Year, Geoff!" I said to myself.

When we next saw each other, after a few minutes, it had been long enough to feel calm again. Not quite as relaxed as we had been before, but talking to each other wasn't difficult, it had just become a bit more businesslike.

"I'd better take you back to Lewes, don't you think? I'm working again at 6 tonight, but I'm quite happy to leave now, it's not that far," Sally looked at me in honest appraisal.

"That would be great," I replied.

On the way to the car, I noticed it was already light, but the kind of wintery grey light that seems to often punctuate dull winter days in Sussex. I was going home to - what exactly? I didn't know but it no longer scared me. There was a spring back in my step that had been lost for many weeks. Luckily I was no longer feeling any ill-effects after the night of misuse of alcoholic beverages. Thought it might be better in the future to drink for pleasure, rather than out of desperation.

Sally had a Mini, a fitting car in her position, I thought while getting into it. I had virtually no memory of the previous evening, so had no idea of the make, let alone model that she drove. It was none too easy to get into, I noticed now that I was sober. My copy of '1984' was on the back seat, so Sally had indeed taken care of it. The 15 minute journey was over way too quickly for my taste. The roads were fairly empty, it was a Saturday, as well as the first day of the new year, but I would happily have spent hours sitting next to her while she drove me through the countryside.

Our conversation was unforced, but it was about nothing in particular. How long she'd had the car, fuel consumption and petrol prices, how rewarding she found it to work with handicapped children and she asked me about my life and career prospects. I told her I was between jobs, but seriously thinking about freelancing in photography, as well as explaining how dedicated I had been to drumming and playing music with my mates. We touched on the fact that I hadn't played with them for several months, which seemed not to surprise her. We exchanged phone numbers, I scribbled hers down on a notebook she had in the glove compartment and tore out the page, then did the same with my own, coupled with an apology that my number was for a phone on the landing, where it was almost impossible to have a private conversation.

She smiled at this, probably because I was suggesting we might have something private to talk about.

"You'll need one of those mobile phones I would think, if you're serious about going freelance." I'd thought of that too, a major expense to think about. Arriving at my flat she got out first and had a look up and down the three floor block that I called home.

"Doesn't look like a bad place to live."

"No, it's not. Haven't been spending so much time here recently, but I will do so soon. Maybe I can show it to you sometime." Sally gave me such an amused look, that we both had to laugh again and it made saying goodbye an easy kiss on the cheeks.

....

My flat was a mess but it was a doddle to clear it up. There was nothing in my fridge, at least nothing without mould on it, and I was wondering where I could get some food. The obvious answer was a 24 hour petrol station, so after clearing up, I made my way to the Esso place about 3/4 mile down the road. I bought some eggs, bacon, milk, tea, some crisps, a bar of chocolate and the last fresh fruit that they had, a couple of bananas and some apples. No, it wasn't very creative and yes, it was quite expensive, but from tomorrow onwards I would start doing things properly. The idea of seriously making a go of photography began to make sense as well as talking to my Mum about what had been going on in my life. I'd also get in touch with my mates Mike and Jay and might suggest getting back together again as a band. As well as going out for a civilised drink from time to time. Maybe it helped that it was the first day of the year.

I found a writing pad that I had been using for jotting down some of my most confusing thoughts and began a to-do list. The first page filled up almost instantly, and the second was half filled before I began to reflect. The London studio had been in the process of changing some of its equipment and modernising. Much of the reasoning was to save on their tax bill, but they had offered most of the staff the chance to buy perfectly good equipment for the same conditions as the retailer was offering in part exchange. I worked out my needs and filled another page with my requirements. It would be way too costly, but I might be able to persuade them to stretch out the repayment. There was some studio flash, I remembered, that would be the first thing. Then I'd need a medium format system with at least three basic lenses. We were working on renewing the background system during my last days there for a motorised, much more sophisticated system, but maybe the wall brackets hadn't been thrown away, I could try and start with them.

I called Mum from the communal phone on the landing and I thought she noticed something had changed. I think she was crying, but tried to stifle it with some long pauses.

"I'm so glad to hear your voice, darling. You sound so well. Happy new year, my love, I do hope we can see you soon."

Although my mother had never been particularly emotional, I never really doubted her love for me, but her enthusiasm made it evident how seriously worried she must have been. People quite close to me had been making an effort to hide their fears about my state of mental health. I even heard Brian's positive reaction in the background, prompted by the change in my Mother's spirits.

Not ashamed about my previous behaviour, now I was so focused on getting my life together that I hadn't give it much thought. I told Mum that I was thinking about starting my own business and she reacted with a really encouraging response. Coming from her, I wondered whether she was clutching at straws, as she didn't always talk in glowing terms about being her own boss. But after speaking for about 10 or 15 minutes, I put down the phone with the intention of calling Mike or Jay next. I hadn't memorised either of their numbers, so I started looking them up in my address book. I was startled when the phone rang and even more surprised when Brian's voice was on the other end.

"Look, old chap, I've come into some money as a maiden aunt of mine died recently…" I started to express my condolences, but he wasn't having any of it.

"I hadn't seen her for years, so don't worry about that. The point is, my divorce is settled and I don't have to share it with my ex if you get my drift."

Well, I got his drift all right, but did wonder whether that was more information than I needed. But he went on.

"I want to offer you an interest-free loan Geoff, I was thinking of about 2500 pounds. What do you think? You can pay back as and when your business allows it."

After Brian's scepticism regarding a career in photography, this was quite a reversal.

"Well thank you very much for the offer, Brian. I mean it's early days still, I'm only starting to make plans but it sounds great."

For a moment I thought he was motivated by guilt, for having moved into my place a few years ago. But then I thought there was so much relief all round that I was finally doing something with my life that it was being encouraged and supported from all sorts of people. After my initial surprise on hearing his plan to move into the flat above the flower shop, I hadn't really felt resentful towards Brian anyway. My attitude had been a bit indifferent really, having been more preoccupied with my own issues than my Mother's.

Brian and I didn't talk for very much longer, I believe he couldn't wait to tell Mum the good news.

I tried Jay next but got no answer. So next I tried Mike's number and Jay answered, which put me off for a moment, but shouldn't have been too much of a surprise. They would hang out together quite often and why not on New Year's Day? Jay was hesitant at first, but I could tell he was willing to give me the benefit of the doubt.

"So, back in the world of the living, are you mate?"

"Yes, you could say that."

It would have been easier to explain face to face about getting drunk, meeting Sally and making a business plan, but he didn't seem to want to probe too much.

"I knew you'd see sense in the end. I wasn't too worried old boy."

He said this in a pseudo posh voice, which I thought was possibly a sign that he was hiding his feelings. He handed over to Mike who sounded much more concerned.

"So what happened, man? Tell me all about it."

I explained I didn't want to go into it over the phone. He was okay with that so we agreed to meet up in Brighton the next afternoon.

....

We met at the Gladstone and having given myself a proper shave and a good shower, I was actually looking more presentable than last time they'd seen me. As expected, they gave me some flak for the last few months.

Mike looked at ease with it all, but I thought Jay was really angry.

"Sorry guys, things haven't been easy since…"

"Since Gerry rejected you!" Jay spat the words at me.

"Gerry was my reason for living!" I complained to them. "She gave my life a meaning!"

"Oh yeah?" Jay questioned me. "So it was nothing to do with her being such a hot looking chick?"

Mike cleared his throat. Jay turned to him,

"I know she's your sister, Mike, but you can still appreciate her looks, can't you?"

"Well, probably, but I never claimed she was reliable."

I think I started to sob at that moment. Yes, partly it was her stunning good looks that I had fallen for and was remembering, but she also made me laugh, she made me feel great. And that was a wonderful feeling. When that went missing I felt alone.

"You are pathetic, Geoff, snap out of it!"

Jay looked really angry and I wanted to snap out of it to stop my friend from ridiculing me. But I'd been in a sad place of my own, where I wanted no-one to reach me and hadn't wanted to reach out either.

"Gerry just isn't very good at relationships. She's got the attention span of a sparrow if a new attraction turns up. She's always been like that. Quite honestly…"

I didn't want to hear the inevitable advice, "…you're better off without her," but he said it all the same. Jay was glaring at me but was obviously trying to control his anger at me.

Mike got up and came back a couple of minutes later with three pints.

"Thanks, Mike, you're a good friend."

"Don't get emotional again, mate, I can't take it." Now he was looking at me quite sternly.

"Get your life together again or you're going to become quite a pain!"

"He already is, Mike," Jay added, helpfully.

But we chatted more over beer about how friends should be there for each other and I asked for a bit of time to get my life back together and we would make music again.

"How much longer do you bloody need?" Jay demanded.

Mike was more soothing saying we needed to be patient with each other and I could have more time if I needed it. He generously offered the use of the rehearsal room as long as I needed it, but said they might turn up any time, that was a risk I'd have to deal with. Soon afterwards, I left the pub, and as no-one followed me, it was clear that they wanted to chat without me.

....

Jay and Mike had both managed to find work after our studies. Mike, inevitably, had got a job working at the stage event management, musical instruments and electronics store in Portslade where he'd worked part-time while studying. Sound systems, amplifiers, musical equipment generally and PA systems were his forte. It was also a great way to get gigs, he had said at lunchtime. Jay started working for an ad agency in Brighton as a junior art director and was doing work for some quite prestigious companies. Although both seemed content with the jobs they had, they were also keen to start playing gigs again.

It took me nearly two hours to get to Portslade. The second day of the year and it was raining, and no surprises there, so I was glad I was wearing my winter jacket. There's something oddly comforting about the sudden force of the wind from the Channel, when you walk along the seafront of Brighton and Hove. It's connected to my idea of home, in a way. Visitors would react as if it was taking their breath away but locals take it all in their stride, apparently hardly noticing it. I was becoming open for other thoughts, I noticed, when I turned the key in the lock in Portslade. Our rehearsal room was accessible through the main entrance of the shop where Mike worked, but it was necessary to deactivate the alarm system as soon as you got in. Otherwise the security agency would come round to see what was happening. That, Mike had assured me, could be really expensive. He had set up a couple of lights to make sure you didn't slip over things in our back room, and switching them on, I decided I'd leave it like that, rather than turning on a ceiling full of fluorescent lighting. I made my way to my drum kit and sat down, grabbing first of all the brushes that I seldom used and got myself into a bluesy, soft mood in order to find my way back to more familiar ground.

The drumsticks and hi-hat brought me back to a world that I felt part of. I was connecting again, back on familiar ground and pounding the skins with power and possibly some beginning of distancing myself from misery.

I listened to music on Mike's professional headphones and beat out my drumming in time to it, or improvising something new. The store had a great collection of demo LPs, CDs and tapes and I played material with Billy Cobham, Gene Krupa, John Bonham, Ringo or Keith Moon. Listening to the apparent simplicity of Ringo's drumming, I'd always thought it was the key to the Beatles swing. The energy of Keith Moon or John Bonham really inspired me, it was trying to get my head round these guys and understand how to express myself and my energy through the beat, rhythm and speed that I was again finding access to. Getting off my stool to get something to drink, I almost tripped over a stand on the way out. I grabbed the nearest solid object for support, and it turned out to be a very sturdy and professional VHS recorder, that kept me from falling flat on my face. On my way back from the kitchen with a glass of water in my hand I realised I had inadvertently turned it on and it was running a video of Ozzy Osbourne playing with his band at some festival. Randy Castillo was the drummer and he really grabbed my attention. I fast-forwarded to Randy's solos and watched this exceptional performer with fascination.

Yes, I had heard of Randy before, but only vaguely and I wasn't a fan of heavy metal at the time. I liked bands such as The Police, Pink Floyd, The Stranglers, Bowie, and I thought R.E.M. were pretty cool, or Nirvana. But I was transfixed in front of the screen with Randy creating this pure energy with the beat of his drums. You could feel him reach out to those areas in your mind and body that you weren't aware of, opening passages of your being that had been asleep for all your life but were now awakening. What was it? How did he do it?

I replayed the tape, probably 4 or 5 times that evening. I thought I might be getting obsessed, but I needed to get to the bottom of this. He was opening up something native, indigenous, that had a rhythm and power that went way beyond his technical skills, (which were excellent, as it happens). I speculated about all sorts of things and began writing them down. I wasn't quite sure of his roots, but believed there was some Native American and Mexican presence in there, both of which suggested a strong connection to the Earth. Thoughts like that were coming into my head, things I had never previously thought about, so I thought it best to write them down. He might have been able to tap into something that is given to us through the vibrating Earth itself, but because of our antiseptic lives we ignore them, or never become aware of them. This was weird, I had never thought of stuff like this in my life. But Randy was sharpening my awareness, one way or another.

4. On My Own

In no way had I forgotten Gerry, the guys and certainly not Sally, but as I was at a bit of a crossroads, I researched Randy's drumming and biography as much as I could, my plans to go freelance were just on hold for a few days. If we'd had access to the Internet in 1994, it would have been so much easier, but I visited the public library, went to record stores and Mike's employer, who was a good source of knowledge too. They had a whole collection of biographies of various stars, some forgotten, some very much still with us. It wasn't easy, but I did eventually find out that he had a strong Apache background, which I thought was incredibly romantic. I borrowed a couple of library books, such as "Bury my heart at Wounded Knee", the one I remember best, as it was a true eye-opener compared to the Hollywood stories we had been told.

This was all keeping me alive and kicking, and itching to try out new drumming skills, which I was practicing almost every day. I wanted to talk to Sally about it, but imagined she might think I was indeed a little obsessed, so I let a week go by before getting in touch again.

When I called her, she seemed genuinely surprised to hear from me. We met up for a coffee in Lewes. I think she thought an afternoon would be less intimidating than an evening date after our first meeting. We both felt some hesitation to begin with, but after a while it was easily overcome. Sally was content not to question me directly about the gaps in my life. We went for a long walk over the downs afterwards and agreed to meet up as often as we could. Sally was so different from Gerry and the difference was bringing me back home. I'd been finding it so hard to get over Gerry, but I knew that's what I had to do but it wouldn't be fair to start a new relationship on the basis of solving an old problem, so we took it slowly. I did speak to Sally in a limited way about my relationship with Gerry and its abrupt end. Perhaps Sally and I would grow together and fill each other's vacuums, as she described it. It was hard to imagine she might have a vacuum to fill. My gratitude towards her behaviour that New Year's Eve was something she shrugged off, saying the time was right for me to move on. She just happened to be there. I wanted to be there for her in a similar way.

As it happens, Sally's support was mainly practical, to begin with. My ideas for setting up a business were taking shape and Jay gave me my first job before I even had the equipment to complete it. I begged and borrowed stuff from friends and my former employer in London, who was keen to move some of their equipment sooner rather than later. Brian's loan would come in handy, and Mum announced she needed a new van for her shop and would I like hers? I suspected she had brought her car plans forward a year or so to support me but didn't want to admit it. It was a Nissan something or other and about the right size for photographic equipment or a drum kit. Support came from people everywhere, there must have been relief all round that I was getting my life back together. I slowly began making a bit of a local name for myself with photographs at Sally's school, weddings, christenings, portraits or advertising jobs that Jay would put my way. Mike came up with the promised gigs, which sometimes made wedding photography a bit awkward so I had to juggle things carefully. But although I was back playing music with Jay and Mike, I knew I had to tell them about my need to move on, preferably with both of them.

....

On one occasion, I remember in the back room of some anonymous country pub, the singer, whose name I can't recall, was singing,

Took a walk and passed your house late last night

All the shades were pulled and drawn way down tight…..

with such a lack of enthusiasm, that I expected there would be boos from the audience. The truth was they were indifferent, nobody was really listening, but it made me realise crunch time was coming. I suggested we meet up the next day, a Sunday, for a serious chat. They agreed and we met at the King and Queen, of all places.

"I've been working on my drumming quite a lot," I explained, "and I'd like to break fresh ground."

Both nodded and Mike said,

"Well, we had noticed that. We were kind of waiting for some kind of input from you. So, where would you like to go? We'd be happy to give up our cover band gigs too."

The music scene was forever changing and I didn't feel part of any kind of movement until the advent of Death Metal, a genre that had its origins in the hard rock of the 60s and 70s but had moved on in its own way. I looked at the various bands and what they were up to as well as the Scandinavian scene and its own rivalries, for example between Norwegian and Swedish bands. In my innocence, I felt attracted to that Scandinavian niche. Explaining this to them was easier than I had expected and they both readily agreed to try it out. I didn't tell them about my research into native earth connections - I thought they would wonder what had happened to me.

So we finally came up with a name, the meaning of which was beyond us, but it felt about right: Valhalla Victims. We had a vague idea about the meaning of Valhalla for Norsemen, and felt that victimhood was always a good start for a band into aggressive complaining and shouting about the injustices of this world. The beginning of the new millennia was slowly approaching, so we thought changing our direction would be a good thing.

Discussing this over a couple of pints, the name having arrived by itself in a way, we all agreed to it, for reasons we couldn't really explain but felt content with. The idea that it was two V-signs for the British public and sounded Scandinavian for anyone else seemed about right. We'd never played Death Metal at all, but were fascinated by the idea of speed, chord changes and growling, to put it in a nutshell. It meant driving the band with my new drumming skills. The demands on stamina and strength were much higher than simple drumming standards to 4/4 time. What did we know? We convinced ourselves we could play anything and the idea of taking anything too seriously wasn't on our agenda anyway. Yes, maybe there were bands out there who were into the real Satanic stuff, but not us. We wanted to write our own compositions and get on the stage and have a good laugh. With our audience, not at our audience, I hasten to add. Of course, there was one weakness to this plan: we didn't have a frontman.

I remember Mike looking into his beer,

"Not a problem guys. I'll put a notice up in the shop and we can have auditions on a Saturday. My boss will let us use the rehearsal room, you'll see, we will have the talents of the county come to our place once the word gets out."

Jay and I glanced at each other with an 'If you say so' look and so we all said "Cheers!" as our pint glasses met with a satisfying clatter over the table. We also realised we were going to have to change our image somewhat. Jay and Mike would need to grow their hair, mine was thinning so I was thinking about shaving it off completely. We discussed make-up (possibly) masks (probably not) leather (you bet) a logo (Jay's job) and kept off the subject of our frontman. I believe we were all a bit concerned about finding someone suitable. We had been together for about five years. Jay and I had been mates for about fifteen. Is there likely to be anyone out there who could lead us? With our idiosyncratic ways and daft conversations, our hysterical outbursts that no-one else understood? We decided to give ourselves a month to find a suitable candidate.

5.Valhalla Victims

Mike announced that he would be holding an audition on the first Saturday in April from about midday at the shop. The shop stayed open on Saturdays till just after lunchtime so I thought he was possibly speculating that other customers might hear what was going on in the rehearsal room and it would pique their interest too. He was being a bit smug and secretive about it all and said he would be choosing the most suitable candidate if we couldn't make it in time. As it happens, I had a wedding shoot in the morning but I thought I could make it around tea-time.

"Perfect," Mike said, smiling and giving Jay a knowing look. "So let's say 5 pm."

Jay looked puzzled but unworried. I was just puzzled. Mike had his own way of doing things and what choice did we have apart from going along with his ideas? I certainly didn't have any and Jay had been too busy to bother. We both knew that all the local talent would eventually come to the store where he worked if they needed any help with advice or equipment and Mike knew almost everything about gear and acoustics. He had much better access to musicians than we did, and he had told us that all the signs he had put up with tear off contact details had been rendered empty after a couple of days. The next two sheets went the same way after another week. So we were in for a wide choice, apparently.

But in reality, by the time I turned up, there weren't many candidates left. Jay was looking a bit despondent, having got to Portslade about half an hour before I did.

"Not impressed with what we've heard so far," he told me in the knowledge that it was a front man we were looking for. Our voice.

"Not an easy exercise!"

Mike breezed in with a steaming mug of coffee looking very cheerful.

"Hey guys, glad you've both arrived. This is Patrick, he's about to sing for us next."

"Hi Patrick", we both greeted this very young looking guy who was walking in just behind Mike and shook his hand. I for one was pretty sure we wouldn't be choosing him, but I was prepared at least to give him a chance in any case. So he stepped up to the two microphones, one for the acoustic guitar slung around his neck and one for his voice. The sound was brilliant, we both thought, but then Mike, our very own perfectionist, would have made sure of that.

He was playing the unmistakable introduction to 'Here comes the Sun'. Now in my book, the Beatles were a great band and George Harrison a personal favourite, but what about our Death Metal idea? He started to sing and even got George's accent right, we had to give him the credit for that. I exchanged looks with Jay, his bemused look reflecting my own, but our instincts told us both not to interfere.

'Little darling, it seems like years since it's been here

'Here comes the sun, here comes the sun

'And I say it's all right....'

Patrick continued and then stopped for a split second. At that moment, I know I was mentally completing the refrain, *'Sun, sun, sun, here it comes'* and I think Jay was too. But we were in for quite a surprise. This boyishly sweet voice and clean acoustic plucking gave way to a much accelerated tempo, some alarming growling and violent guitar slashing.

'Sun, sun, sun, here it comes,' had never sounded so scary, but it was great, we loved it! It made us laugh and toss our heads around. Yes, it was just about recognisable as the Beatles song, but Patrick owned it. Like buying a secondhand classic car and tuning it so extravagantly that the original marque was becoming hard to trace. We almost fell into a laughing fit, because we realised that we could be on to something and this was the perfect explanation for Mike's somewhat secretive behaviour. My drum set was in the corner and I joined in to support him. This young kid gave me a sort of manic grin and motioned for Jay to pick up the guitar that was leaning next to an amp.

We jammed away at *'Here comes the Sun'* for several minutes and revelled in every moment of it. If this was Death Metal I loved it. Mike was fiddling about with some switches and gained a bit of echo and feedback effect too. He was also recording it and when we came to the last notes and I crashed the cymbals to a final crescendo, he flicked the switch to play the tape back to us.

But first we savoured the moment and gave him a signal to wait. This was such a new experience, the energy that was buzzing in Mike's office was completely different and much better than playing covers had ever been. We had so many questions to ask Patrick, we didn't want to overwhelm him, but they kept coming.

"Where did you learn that?"

"Have you played in other bands?"

"Where did you get that voice?"

"Yeah, I want one like that!"

On and on we went, talking nonsense but enjoying the presence of this kid who was maybe going to make our dreams come true. He was confident, yet also quiet with us, respectful even.

Meanwhile Mike put the tape back on and it came through the loudspeakers with the clarity of live music. We listened for a couple of minutes, but when it became irresistible, even Mike picked up a bass and we all jammed on top of the improvised recording. We had the time of our lives. Patrick was Eric Burdon, Steve Winwood and a growler like the Swedish Johan Hegg all rolled into one. He growled with unbelievable ease and yet had a boyish appearance that looked anything but threatening. We would indeed all have to work on our appearance, as none of us looked anything like as scary as we should have.

"Let's got to the Anchor for a beer," Mike suggested.

"Are you old enough for that?" Jay asked Patrick.

"Sure, I was 18 last month," Patrick replied, giving Mike a look. Mike gave him a look back but didn't object. Knowing his attention to detail I had no doubt that he had written down Patrick's date of birth. But if we were taking a minor out for a drink, I didn't want to know too much, so decided against pursuing the matter. As it happens, there was no need for concern, as Patrick only ordered an apple juice when we got there. The other two went for beer, as did I, confident in the knowledge that one beer would be okay.

So we had a long and animated discussion about where we wanted the band to go, how we would compose our own material, how much we could depend on Patrick, who was still at school, soon to take his A levels. It turned out he was from Worthing, where he lived alone with his dad. His Mother had died in a hit and run accident he told us without much emotion. But he probably had had a fair amount of practice and become immune to emotional depths when recalling the facts of his loss.

"My Da works for a pharmaceutical company," Patrick told us. 'Da' was the only clue he gave to his Irish roots, apart from his name. His way of speaking sounded typical for our area.

"But he's a musician too. Plays a whole lot of stuff, guitar, piano, sax, even trumpet if he has to. My Mum and Da used to sing together in Irish bands, folky stuff and traditional Irish. My Da can also do a fair impression of Van Morrison, given enough encouragement."

Mike surprised us with the spontaneity of his singing voice and sang,

"Into the mystic…."

"Dab, dab, dabada, dada da."

We all joined in, in quite good harmony, followed by raucous laughter. Of course we knew Van Morrison wasn't Death Metal, but it was cool to find we could work together with the ease of snapping our fingers. A five or six year age difference is quite a lot when you are that young, but we felt we had made a good choice and wanted to make Patrick feel welcome. I felt a particular solidarity towards him, being also the son of a single parent. (At least until recently in my case. I thought about asking if his Dad had a girlfriend but thought better of it.)

Bands often fall apart because of the clash of egos. Patrick was younger than all of us, and didn't seem to have the frontman limelight-grabbing ego that would often lead to a break up. We had hardly got together, but were already talking about the implications. Patrick wanted to study architecture from September, which he could do at Brighton's Uni. He had a gig that evening so he took his leave and the three of us were left to chat about where this project was going to go. In some ways, we felt we weren't legitimate Death Metallers, as we really didn't know much about it and just enjoyed playing around with it. We laughed about becoming more scary, both Jay and Mike felt they couldn't look too crazy or they would end up scaring the people they met in their day jobs. I needed to think about that too. As a student, and our frontman, Patrick would have much more freedom to walk around with shoulder length hair and a wispy beard if he wanted to.

We rehearsed after our first meeting twice a week, Mondays and Thursdays, at the usual rehearsal room at Mike's workplace. Having listened to as much drumming as I could I knew it was going to be a lot more strenuous to pay than standard hit covers. But I found the rehearsals exhilarating and always looked forward to getting together with the others.

Sally couldn't take it. She came to one of our first rehearsals, mostly out of curiosity, but had to go outside after a couple of minutes.

"It's just so loud and tuneless," Sally explained, "It hurts my eardrums to be that close up as well."

But she would never have wanted me to stop and was quite tolerant of the whole idea. She also made friends with Jay's girlfriend, Chrissie, and they would sometimes come along just to meet up and go out to a movie or something while we practiced.

....

One Saturday, Jay turned up looking pleased with himself. We waited for him to reveal his secret and it turned out he'd been working on our logo. He had prepared himself as if he was going to pitch an important project to a big customer.

"So, here's the thing," he began. "I'll show you the result in a moment, but first I want to explain a bit about where we are culturally and historically."

"What?" Mike responded with a wave of his hands. "We aren't in need of a history lesson, we just want a cool logo!" Patrick giggled and I had to intervene. I knew Jay wouldn't give us a history lesson if there wasn't some relevance to it.

"Shut up you two! Let's see what Jay's done, okay?" They both shrugged and Jay looked at me.

"Thank you Geoff, for restoring a sense of decorum." Patrick and Mike laughed again at this mock presentation, but Jay was good at it, no doubt about it. He'd probably learned as much in his new job.

"Right. The logo is based on Celtic symbolism." He looked at our puzzled faces but went on,

"Celtic symbolism is more or less standard for the metal scene. This is where it comes from: our little island was Celtic before the Normans came over in 1066 and the Celts moved mostly to the outer reaches of our islands, to Scotland, Ireland and Wales. This led to culture mixes we had never previously experienced. I used the Celtic Knot as a basis for the design, and, I hear you ask, what about the Scandinavian question?"

As it happens, that was exactly what I was going to ask.

"The Goths are Scandinavian and come from the island of Gotland. They adapted the visual language of the Celts, mostly owing to the influence of the Christian monks who regularly came over from Ireland to convert them. So what I am about to show you has a relevance to our name with the two vees, and the Celtic Knot which was a ubiquitous symbol of the time."

With that, Jay lovingly untied the strings to his black portfolio, and in a moment where I felt a drumroll might have been appropriate, removed the protective layer to expose his Celtic Knot, our logo.

The effect wasn't immediate at all. All three of us bent over to look at the design that he had printed out in A3, while Jay took a step back. Patrick was the first to speak.

"Man, I think that's really cool." I looked across to Mike who smiled, nodding in agreement.

"It would look brilliant on teeshirts!"

"And the colour is pretty cool, too," I added. "The genius of graphic design wins the day, don't you think, guys?" Jay gave us a look of mock embarrassment but he did look pleased.

"Gentlemen, I believe you have made the right decision," speaking in his business pitching mode.

"In fact, I was so confident that it was the right design, that I haven't bothered with alternatives, contrary to my usual practice."

"You're such a bluffer, Jay! Such a bloody genius bluffer!" Mike had an odd way of expressing himself sometimes, but Jay knew how it was meant and a subsequent man hug confirmed his appreciation. I gave him one too, then Patrick went to shake his hand as our newcomer he was probably feeling somewhat shy, but Jay gave him the full treatment with a bear hug. I think despite everything, he was quite relieved that we liked his work and it hadn't been a hard sell.

The sooner we got those teeshirts made, the better. Slowly but surely, we were becoming a real entity, a recognisable Death Metal rock band.

....

We spent well over four months practicing until we thought we had honed our skills and written enough material to go out on the road. By late September we were ready to try an open air festival in Hampshire, just to test the water, so to speak.

The band was well received, we were the second act on stage when it was getting dark which was good for us and our material.

We started with a number that Mike and Patrick had jointly written, *'Hell has no fury'*. Heads started banging pretty much from the beginning. Patrick had grown a beard to hide behind and his hair was straggly and long, so he was looking quite the part. He now had an undefinable age. Our encore was "Here comes the Sun". It was welcomed by a few jeers to begin with, particularly as we had kept to the acoustic intro, but when Patrick started growling to it, the crowd moved like a Mexican wave, only faster. They loved it. We thought we could hardly have got on to a better start.

....

After our first gig we played in a few festivals around the country, never earning very much but enjoying ourselves, pretty much, at every gig. We would go to places like Belgium, Scandinavia, Holland or Northern France over the years, Ireland on a few occasions and Scotland from time to time, but mainly in the summer months when our jobs would allow time off. Sometimes we'd play in pubs, locally or at least reachable in a couple of hours. It wasn't a full-time job by any means but it was vitally important to us all, it was our common passion. We had a modest international following and they seemed to be a loyal group of people, often coming backstage to say Hi. Our repertoire wasn't great in numbers, but it was big enough to fill most slots we were offered and no-one complained - to me at least - that we didn't have new material every year. We were in a position similar to many bands who didn't make it big-time. Music was more than a hobby but less than a job, more a passion really, a situation we were quite content to live with as we went about our daily lives.

....

Sally and I got married in 1999. My proposal was a bit casual, mainly because I was embarrassed (yes, also in case she said no) and certainly didn't feel the inclination to go down on one knee! We were out walking on the downs, with a view towards the distant sea in one direction and otherwise surrounded by the Weald countryside. By this time, we had been going out together for nearly 5 years but I hadn't thought I could ask her until I was fairly confident that I could support her if necessary. It was May and the sun was deciding whether or not to shine or hide behind the clouds. We had been talking about all sorts of things, but had run out of conversation all of a sudden. Now Sally is the easiest person in the world to have a conversation with, so when she stopped talking, I asked her what was wrong.

"Nothing. Why do you ask?" She said that with such a provocative smile, that it made me a bit lost for words, and as I had been planning to ask her to marry me that afternoon, I think her intuition must have picked up on it and this made me more than a little nervous. I mean, we had been living together for so long, so it shouldn't have been such a big deal, but I think Sally was having a good laugh at my discomfort.

"Well, I wanted to ask you..."

"Yes," she answered with a broad smile on her face, "go on." At that moment, May decided to behave more like April and a cold breeze blew across the downs and we even heard thunder in the distance. Within a few seconds it was pelting down with rain. A few minutes beforehand we had passed by a tree and now we both had the same idea, to head for it and shelter under its protection. We rushed down the hill towards it and reached it, out of breath and rather wet. Sally was shivering by this time and I was feeling cold too, so our only comfort was to hold onto each other as tightly as we could.

Her blue eyes looked up at mine and despite the shivering, kept me focused on the subject in mind.

"You were saying, Geoff?" Her teeshirt was wet through, but she wasn't prepared to allow me to change the subject. So I gave up and just said,

"Sally, please marry me! Would you?" Her eyes and her teeth were sparkling in the sunshine and rain as I looked over her shoulder for a rainbow, expecting to see one at that moment, but if there was one somewhere, I couldn't locate it. Sally thought I wasn't paying attention.

"Well, do you want to know my answer or not?" She shook me as if in annoyance, though she was obviously playing around.

"I was just seeing if there was a rainbow anywhere." I protested.

"I see. So you were thinking about taking pictures?"

"No. I just thought it would be romantic." And before things got out of hand, she drew me even closer, and said,

"Of course I'll marry you. Why ever not?"

....

I loved her as I still do, we decided to get married the same year and at our wedding reception Patrick and his dad played Irish music, which was great, even allowing for the huge jump in style for Patrick. We were particularly honoured when he and Jack sang their version of Van Morrison's 'Into the Mystic.' Mike was looking a bit worse for wear, but determined to help out, so he joined in the chorus, and considering his alcohol consumption, his rendition of *'Dab, dab, dabada, dada da,'* was more than acceptable.

We wanted to have children but it wasn't to be. I know Sally was very disappointed - she would have been the world's best Mum, but we also knew our lifestyle would have been restricted by children. She wanted me to be happy above all. Sally's generous spirit put my interests before hers, even though I wanted to make sure she got what she wanted out of life as well. But her satisfaction was still in teaching kids less fortunate than ourselves. We talked about it less than we thought about it, although there were times when we had a proper heart to heart about being childless. On one occasion, I'd felt quite moved by her.

"I've got a boy called Gavin in my second year class. His mother was apparently a drug addict and he had a stroke when he was 5 or 6. As you can imagine, when a child has a stroke, it profoundly affects development. As it was he hadn't had an easy start and was living in a care home from very early on. The stroke seemed to arrest the development that he had had, some capabilities such as speech were lost or starkly reduced and I gave him some speech therapy to improve his communication skills.

"It was a huge effort for him to relearn, and he would sometimes stamp his foot in frustration. One day, a sentence we'd been practicing for a while came out perfectly. It was something like 'I want to play football with the other boys.' He beamed at me in triumph and threw his arms around my neck and hugged me so hard it almost hurt.

"And at that moment I realised I am a mother for my children, even if they aren't my biological kids at all. It's made it so much easier to accept our situation, Geoff." She gave me a look loaded with so much empathy that I wondered what I had done to deserve her.

Not for the first time, I also wondered if I hadn't been a biological father and had never found out about it. Geraldine and I had not been in contact at all and despite my regular contact with her brother Mike he never spoke about her and I never asked.

Sally also continued to help her uncle and cousin at the pub in Lewes when they needed the support. She loved me with a selflessness that I sometimes found hard to match. We'd moved out of her flat into a cottage, also near Uckfield where she looked after the garden with devotion and attention to detail. I just enjoyed sitting in it, if pressed I'd mow the lawn. Sally loved the wild flowers that would grow in the lawn, so fortunately, that didn't happen too often.

My photographic business was going quite well, partly thanks to Jay's support in advertising and family portraits that were in demand. Then in the early 2000s, I had to make a snap decision about going digital and did so as quickly as possible, which for a while gave me an advantage over some of the competition. When almost everyone went digital after about 2008, I had a bit of a tough time as people were catching up while spending a lot less. I was still fascinated by the enhanced speed of digital photography and found it preferable to spending nights in a darkroom to achieve a result which, frankly, was easier to attain and repeat with computer technology.

Jay became senior art director and he also kept the firm running smoothly. He kept his hair cut short and wore wigs on stage. Jay and Chrissie had two children, a boy and a girl ahaving got married about a year after us. They went through quite a crisis and divorce was looking imminent for a while, but after some new-age therapy, found a way to keep their relationship going. (His words, not mine.)

An offer of partnership in the electronics company kept Mike from leaving it. So much depended on him - his knowledge and expertise were second to none. He also embraced modern technology, which his boss had given up on, and this made his continuing employment essential for the good of the company. Mike had plenty of admiring girlfriends and seemed unwilling to commit himself to just one of them.

Patrick's career flourished from building project to building project. He had a passion for it and a part-time lecturer recognised his talent while he was still at college. He was also offered a partnership, which he turned down, unwilling to limit his options. He has been together with his girlfriend Mary since his mid 20s. His voice still had the same range it had when we first met and clients seem to tolerate his appearance. Patrick would never be a candidate for a wig.

We were really just a bunch of friends who enjoyed hanging out with each other and playing the music that kept us entertained. It was after a gig that we would really appreciate how thoroughly therapeutic Death Metal was, but it was unlikely that we, or anyone else, would have talked about it in that way. The exhaustion was like a marathon run and the euphoria that came after the finishing line. I didn't need a gym, my biceps were quite impressive, though I say so myself.

At the end of the first decade of the new century, we made a life-changing discovery. Although it had been going since the early 1990s, we hadn't heard about the small village of Wacken in Northern Germany until about 2010. We went over as audience members first. Patrick and Mary had been in 2009 and insisted we came with them the following summer. Mary was the only Metaller among our partners and was at least as enthusiastic as Patrick. They both wore leather jackets with the festival name emblazoned on them.

6.A visit to Germany

We arrived for 3 days of heavy metal in a village that opened its doors to all sorts of weird and wonderful people in August 2010. Patrick had lent us his DVD of "Full Metal Village" and various live recordings at Wacken and we were looking forward to it like kids at Christmas. Such a strange combination of a sleepy rural village which had embraced our kind of music, and well organised German structure. People from all over the world came to this musical Mecca. And from many walks of life, bankers, teachers, policemen and policewomen, students from Australia or Brazil, every category of human being seemed well represented. The inhabitants were big fans too, and made an effort that we should all enjoy ourselves, while offering souvenirs or food and drinks for sale in their front gardens.

Some big names were there, Mötley Crüe, Iron Maiden, Slayer and others, but we went more for the less well known bands playing on the smaller stages, of which there was quite a choice. Patrick and Mary had made friends with one of the bands the previous year, and were both invited up on stage to jam with them. At this point we realised that Mary was Patrick's best kept secret, she could growl and scream with unrivalled energy, just like her boyfriend. Inevitably, there were people there who knew Mike from the shop and fairly quickly we made contact with the organisers to negotiate for a gig in 2011. Valhalla Victims as a name seemed to convince them quickly that we would deliver the goods they appreciated.

All of us, apart from Patrick, were now approaching our forties but we felt as if we were starting over again. We wrote new material, practiced older songs that we hadn't played for a long time and spent the 12 months coming up to Wacken Open Air focused on this one particular gig. Wacken is not Woodstock, but in its own way it also produces three days of love, peace and music. Our wives and girlfriends agreed to come with us, although both Sally and Chrissie reserved the right to visit nearby Hamburg and not slide in Wacken's mud for every one of the three days. By the time August 2011 came round, we had already played more gigs that year as a result of our upcoming appearance there. We rubbed shoulders with some veterans of the Metal scene and it felt like our spiritual home to be there in Northern Germany and absorb the atmosphere that was confusing for some and a therapeutic experience for many others.

The heavy metal scene was like a village in itself, the word, once out there, would travel quickly and we were invited to Brighton Fringe and some smaller festivals, locally and nationally. Our new found fame was profitable too, we actually earned a reasonable amount of money on the road and found that even after expenses we could waltz to the bank with a spring in our step.

Even Jay, wary about being recognised by clients from his advertising connections, began collecting fans from the very source from which he had hoped to stay anonymous. We were blessed with a loyal following and a group of supporters who helped us on the road. Patrick's father Jack, now retired, offered to take over management and road management and we agreed in the knowledge that he could be trusted more than strangers who would make us dubious but unrealistic offers. He had a good business sense and was equally protective towards us all.

Mike often had to deal with fans, ostensibly interested in guitars or amps, but actually more interested in his autograph. It was amazing to be confronted by people who had so much knowledge of us and our personal history, much of which was to be found at various internet sites, having made it their business to record every trivial fact they could. All of us were tempted to give up our day jobs, but resisted in the knowledge that the metal scene, though loyal and generous, was still only a small part of the whole music scene and if there happened to be a dip in our fortunes, which there undoubtedly would be at some point, it would throw our lives into utter chaos.

As a bunch of rock musicians, we were almost as disciplined and conservative as classical musicians. Yes, we all liked beer, except for Patrick who was more of a wine drinker, but our experiments with drugs were few and far between. We all had proper jobs, although it was often a struggle to juggle all our obligations with devotion equal to our enthusiasm for Death Metal. It was serious fun for us all and we rarely had proper arguments with each other, on or off the stage. We decided against making our anger about wars in Iraq and Afghanistan the focus of new compositions and kept to a more general aggression and vitality about life and all its complicated connections.

Wacken was keen on having us back every so often and we had already had quite a following there. We were hoping to be booked for one of the larger stages next time around. In fact it got to the point where Patrick could remove the mic and point it to the crowd, confident in the knowledge that they'd fill in the lyrics to chant 'Hell has no fury' or another one of our popular numbers. Sales of CDs were in steep decline except on such occasions, where Jack would make a killing. The funds he collected from the sales of CDs and merchandise went towards our expenses, so we didn't need to dip too deeply into our own funds.

We were incredibly lucky, in that our success was enough to make it worth the effort, but not that big to make our day jobs impossible to carry out. Patrick was still in demand as a studio musician, while his reputation as a regional architect was growing continually. Jay was offered a post as director and partner in the design company which he had gladly accepted. In a similar way, Mike's former boss had retired, leaving him in charge, while retaining 51% ownership himself.

7. Wacken 2017

So this was going to be the biggest headline gig for us ever! Going on just before Alice Cooper was enough to mobilise our little Sussex army of fans, including Brian and Judy (that's my Mum), Brian's daughters Helen and Rachel (both of whom were now grown up women and much easier to talk to) with their partners, 8 of Patrick and Jack's relations from Belfast and Derry, seemingly Mike's whole family (apart from Gerry) and current German girlfriend Uschi, Jay's wife Chrissie, their children and other friends. Jay's sister Jenny even dragged her husband to join in the fun as well. Enough people in fact, to hire a bus to take everyone across to Wacken. Some were prepared to sleep in tents, others preferred the shuttle bus and the comfort of a Hamburg hotel.

We all wanted to go with them, but it wasn't possible, we needed too much space for ourselves and it would have been a logistical nightmare with all the hardware we had with us and musical instruments. We had a truck take everything over and followed by plane. Landing in Hamburg, we hired a car but remained in constant contact with the Valhalla bus through various chat and video connections. It was obvious they were determined to have a great time, and started enjoying themselves before they'd even left the country.

When it was finally our turn to play we were already on the stage without having created much awareness from the crowd. One of those magic moments when time seems to stop still, it is almost silent and the public is recovering from the impact made by the last act and stage fright kicks in before the adrenalin rush. The M.C. announces us,

"Ladies and Gentleman, let's give a true Wacken welcome to Valhalla Victims!" A roar came up from the crowd, as my double foot pedals introduced our first number that many would recognise, a recent composition that had been popular at most of our recent gigs, *'A drop in the ocean of time'*. I have to hit the bass drum at tremendous speed, at least compared to most of the other intros, but it's a great way to get started and it got our adrenalin flowing immediately.

I have to say, we played our hearts out. Patrick was in fantastic form and held the crowd in the palm of his hand, bringing on Mary half an hour before we finished our standard set for a duet that had the whole place rocking. We relished every minute of it. I must have lost 2 or 3 pints of sweat - every time I glanced at my face in the monitor, it seemed to be showing beads of sweat continuously dripping from my forehead. I couldn't keep the water flowing fast enough to replace it. Mike, now alternating between bass and keyboards, gave us a live quality that was explosive in its energy. He was almost acrobatic when he changed from one instrument or keyboard to the next and it sent the crowd screaming. Had to laugh at Jay, here was a 90 minute concert and despite efforts to look stern, I don't think he was ever without a smile on his face. Valhalla Victims were serious stuff, but we were spreading joy at the same time. People were slam-dancing in front of the stage, some even while singing every single word in sync with Patrick. The moshpit was humming with enthusiastic activity, and every so often I lost concentration for a moment when I saw stage divers in danger of falling. The 'double vee' of our band name had also become something of a competitive double hand signal to the horn so often seen on and offstage. The British contingent was easy to recognise, they'd keep both hands extended and the palm outwards, like Churchill's victory sign. People from elsewhere were basically fine with telling us to 'fuck off' but we didn't take that too personally. We couldn't expect everyone to know the ins and outs of British rudeness and anyway, they were banging their heads with such free form aggression, I'm sure they didn't mean it.

And Wacken is such an odd place. We stayed there for a few extra nights, so that I could take some pictures of the dismantling of the stages and scaffolding. Patrick talked to some of the organisers, fascinated by the speed and ease with which they approached everything. Jay interviewed a couple of local people, filmed by Mike with Uschi on hand, in case of translation issues. The local shops, when it was all over, were more than happy to chat with us. The whole village lives basically from these ten days or so. Their stock is always in demand and the whole thing seems to have discouraged residents from leaving for the city. Or slowed the process down, at the very least. Some residents escape from the area and believe that the devil's music has no place in their society. Which we thought was very funny, having never prayed to the devil, let alone ever having asked him to come with us on a gig. It seems to be quite a general misunderstanding about our music, made even worse of course, when we describe it as 'Death Metal'. What a harmless bunch of blokes we are in fact. But we all derive a certain satisfaction and mirth from the fact that we are considered bad boys (or girls) and have satanic followers. Watching 'Rammstein' for the first time, I can understand why you might make that connection. But it's all theatre in the end, just wholesome fun, a bit like watching a horror film of the 80s, if you're in the right frame of mind.

Most people in Wacken have understood this and embrace the idea with earnest passion. They are unassuming people generally, more concerned about the welfare of their cows or how the rain could affect the crops at harvest time. They have a very laid back opinion about the festival and since having the brilliant idea of an underground pipeline for beer - which worked very well - they have been rightly described as legendary.

For Sally, the best part of the festival was talking to local people after it was all over. She really saw how peaceful it all is, and although it wasn't our first time, she felt the love and appreciation of our fans was real.

"If you called it 'Wacken: A Festival of Peace', I doubt as many people would turn up, but that's really what it is. 'Wacken Open

Air' sounds like a warning - the abbreviation 'WOA' - sounds like 'You'd better watch out'. Great marketing. Apparently, although there are lots of big companies who sponsor it now, but I was talking to a guy who was here from the beginning, 1990 I think, and it was just so a few mates could play in a field in front of some friends. Just amazing."

We were walking across a field and it made me quite euphoric to hear how much she enjoyed it. Although she helps at photographic assignments sometimes, and I have often been present for special occasions at her school, we don't share the music scene as much. She always looks glad when Chrissie turns up so they can go off and do something together instead.

We all got home still feeling high. It had been an incredible few days, we had seen and heard a lot of other bands too, it was simply what connected us best. Backstage there's a feeling of equality too, whether you are Megadeth or Vallhalla Victims. The feeling lasts for a good while too, as if your body has been injected with a feel-good vibe.

I had assignments to finish at home and it was evident that word had got out that we were taking the stage with bands like Alice Cooper's and it was obviously making a good impression. I was surprised at how many of my clients were well informed about what we were up to. Most were more than happy to be associated with a Death Metal drummer, in fact, I believe some made quite a point in telling colleagues and family.

I wouldn't say I had ruined my drum kit, but it does need tender loving care from time to time and new skins too. Mike had given me an address that he recommended and I left them my kit, confident that they knew what they were doing.

8. The Accident

Two weeks later I went to pick everything up. Some of the kit looked like new, apart from scratches that I hadn't asked them to get rid of. Scratch removal was a service they also offered, but I felt the scratches and dents were evidence of the personal nature of my kit. I had caused those blemishes, they were part of the life we were experiencing together and I didn't want to lose them.

Sussex Drummers Lab was based north of Brighton, in a small village called Poynings. A quiet idyllic place, it often seemed incongruous to see the mostly leather-clad, long-haired drumming community meet up there. While I was loading my refurbished gear into the van, I was amused to see members of a brass band, still in uniform, unload their drums, as if they'd known the drums would only last for this final performance, after which they would need immediate attention. I couldn't work out any other reason why they would still be in their uniform, unless it was some kind of fetish thing.

With the kit packed in bubble wrap, I carefully placed the items in a compact form and strapped them tightly in the van to be sure there would be no tipping over or sliding about. I was looking forward to when we would begin rehearsing again soon and noticed that I never treated my drum kit this respectfully when we had gigs. My precious cargo had gone up in value, it now held the traces of over 20 years of Death Metal history. And had new skins, so this was treasured stuff, to be protected as best I could. I reversed out of the loading area and turned onto the road beneath the Downs that I knew so well. The weather was beautiful, I seldom got to see the area in its pristine state as we mostly got home in the dark.

A brief look at the fuel gauge confirmed the beep that I'd heard when I turned the engine on. I was now running very, very low. I should just make it to Lewes where there is a choice of petrol stations each side of the railway, about a mile apart. A bit cheaper than the service station in Pyecombe on the A23, I considered, a thought that would have driven Sally mad, if she had been with me. She tended to fill up when the gauge was just below half, whereas I would wait till the warning light went on. We often joked about it, but she sometimes said in seriousness,

"Geoff, one day you are really going to regret that silly habit!"

I just considered stopping more frequently, which is what she did with her car, a waste of time and energy. So I was up on the Downs, confident I'd make it home and easily get to the next service station, when the one I was counting on, Esso, was closed 'owing to alterations'. I knew it wasn't far to the BP on the other side of the tracks, so I made my way to the level crossing, which thankfully, was open.

Then, as if it had been waiting for this moment just to show me, the van stopped right on the tracks, in the middle of the level crossing. Cursing, I got out and began to push. The damn thing would not move! Not an inch. I couldn't think why but kept trying, sweating ever more profusely in the September sun. There was no-one about, the whole place was deserted as if the human race had given up on me. For doing what exactly? Just for being a little too optimistic with my fuel consumption? I hardly think so. So I went back to pushing and shoving when I noticed an emergency beep coming from the barriers. It seemed a train was on its way and I was in the way and the barriers couldn't come down as a result. I panicked and opened the door to try and steer myself out of harm's way. It was then that I noticed the handbrake was on. It's a silly thing they teach you - no doubt with sound reasoning - at driving school, but it had become so automatic, that I hadn't noticed or even thought about looking for some cause for the refusal of the car to budge. By this time I was hearing distant whistling from an approaching train, so as quickly as I could, I gave the van a mighty push, to begin with it had no effect at all, then I noticed that turning the steering wheel really would help, as the front wheel was slightly embedded in one of the track grooves, so, applying a sharp right turn I managed to free the van and push it back towards the road. This seemed to cost me such a superhuman effort, that I needed to grab some breath to fill my muscles with enough energy to get out of harm's way. By this time the whistle was continuous, I heard the scream of breaks and felt an enormous, short and very sharp pain to my head. The van with its valuable cargo had stopped just in front of a hedge, with the wheels slightly in a ditch and I remember thinking, thank goodness - at least it's not damaged.

I went up to the van, largely oblivious to the commotion that was going on by this time and tried to open the door on the driver side. It was then that I realised I didn't have an arm or a hand left with which to open the door. In fact, I didn't have a body at all. Well, this was odd. As if by suction, I was drawn to the front of the train that had stopped a couple of hundred meters further down the track. I found myself looking at it and I examined something that had a rather beautiful structure just below the front window. It was brain, I realised after a while - my brain presumably. The distraught driver was leaning against his door, shaking badly and fussing with a smartphone. I wanted to give him a hand and tell him everything was alright, but hard as I tried, he wouldn't respond.

At this point I had another look at the brain, and came face to face with what had really happened. I was dead. Some while ago, I'd read that near death experiences were caused by the brain and I thought - they should redo that research, I don't have a brain anymore but I'm still here, whatever that means. At the moment of thinking those thoughts another suction effect brought me back to the level crossing. I was looking for my body, it had to be close. There 'I' was, lying in the brambles with part of my head gone, but it was me, or my body at least, of that there was no doubt in my mind. There was also some blood and I had the strange thought when I looked at my damp armpits that I hoped I'd put on enough deodorant that morning. I didn't want the paramedics to turn up their noses when examining me. Then I wondered, do they even send an ambulance when someone has obviously left his mortal coil? Or do the undertakers come and take care of the body? Or the police? I had no idea but intended to hang around a while and find out.

I think that was the moment when it all started to sink in. My thoughts were with Sally and that propelled me straight to her classroom in East Grinstead. She was doing an experiment with bricks, whereby the weight of small wooden bricks had to be balanced by different positioning of the subsequent larger bricks, which involved two or three children working together to make sure the whole thing didn't collapse. I'd seen her do this before, but this time I was absolutely transfixed by the beauty of it. I saw sparks rise and fall, interacting with each other depending on how close the kids were to achieving balance, as if they were actively cooperating with each other, or playing even, as participants in the game. This was so absorbing that I found myself down at the level where it was all happening, but with an enormous change of scale, so that the small bricks took on the size of walls and the flashes and sparks of multi-coloured energy were participating with apparent enjoyment. The fingers of the children were the size of French baguettes and I could see they had their own flashes and sparks, in amazing colours, some of which I don't think I'd seen before, but each child seemed to have a somewhat different set of colours and shapes. This was so cool! I could have spent ages watching this miniature theatre acting out these tiny dramas. Then I saw fingers of a much bigger size, more like a double-baguette. It was unmitigated joy to see this person's hand and recognise her energy as belonging to my loving wife Sally. But the seriousness of what had happened was also sinking in and I felt immensely sad and grew back to my normal size so that I could see her face. When I felt we matched again, I unrealistically tried to kiss her and saw a look of horror cross her face.

Being the professional that Sally has always been, she finished the class and helped the children disperse when the final bell went and she packed her things and left the school as quickly as she could. Before starting the car, I saw her choose my mobile number and call.

"Hello, this is Geoff Kent, I'm sorry I can't take your call at the moment. If you are calling about photography or Valhalla Victims, you've come to the right place. Please leave a short message and your contact number and I will get back to you as soon as I can."

"Hi Geoff, it's me. Just calling to make sure you got your drums back and everything. I'll be home soon and see you later. If you want anything special let me know, I can pick it up on the way home. Otherwise we can finish the roast chicken tonight and I'll just add some salad. We can also finish that bottle of Sauvignon. Bye, love."

'Bye bye love, bye bye sweet caress, hello emptiness, I feel like I could die.'

Death had reached me totally unprepared. I was full of regrets and full of love for Sally and I could see her, I could hear her, I found I could smell her too, I could almost touch her, but I was no longer there to be seen, touched or loved. I was gone. I had no idea what was going to happen next, but I didn't see a white light or a tunnel or any of the other things that you hear about when people come back from the brink of life and death. Obviously a lot had changed since the accident, but my awareness seemed hardly to have changed at all. I was still the same essence, so to speak, experiencing this rather confusing reality. But thoughts were evidently dynamic, because on thinking again about the accident, I was suddenly back at the scene in a single whoosh, taking no time or apparent movement, just hovering above the ordered chaos that emergency services are trained to deal with. I could tell that they were taking care of my body and wondered why. There were valuable organs to be harvested as long as I was still fresh, as it were. In my life I had never been keen on the idea of organ transplants but now I wanted to shout out.

"Go for it guys! Take anything you need. Eyes, heart, liver, kidneys, anyone who needs them is welcome to give mine a try if they are any good!"

Now I wished I had carried an organ donor card in my wallet, but the default position seemed to be if you don't opt out, you're in. I saw my wallet was open in the van and my next-of-kin was being researched on someone's tablet.

"Please visit her." I thought. "I know you're strapped for funds but a phone call would be dreadful. She's just getting some lettuce from the garden to go with the cold roast chicken we had last night."

I needn't have been concerned. A sense of urgency took her home without stopping and police officers made their way to meet her after my body had been taken to a hospital or mortary. I wondered whether they would need an autopsy. Again, my awareness was there at our front door in Uckfield, as I saw the officer approach it with a heavy heart. A female colleague caught up with him and they both stood there while putting off that moment to ring the bell for a long-lasting two or three seconds. Both breathed in deeply, she rang the bell and Sally was there very soon after that with a look that I recognised. It was strength combined with immense sadness and expectation.

"Mrs Kent? I'm afraid we have some serious news. May we come in?"

I saw the guy glance at his colleague for her choice of the word 'serious' but he let it go and Sally let them in without a word and showed them into our kitchen/dining room. Before the officers had time to explain what had happened, Sally, who I could see was trying to avoid talking for fear of crying couldn't help herself.

"He's dead isn't he? My husband Geoff. How did it happen?"

"Yes, I'm afraid so. We can only speculate, but his vehicle was a little way off from the level crossing where it happened, and he was hit by an oncoming train while he was still on the crossing."

Which was a pretty good analysis, I thought. I wondered if they'd had video evidence?

Sally's hand went up to her face and covered her mouth as she sat down onto our leather armchair. I could tell she wanted to wait to cry until they'd left, but was finding it very hard. The well-trained policewoman suggested she made Sally a cup of tea, to which she nodded her assent.

A consummate professional, she seemed to know where everything was. Maybe British homes are more similar than we had thought.

Sally gasped for air, she was evidently trying to ask a question, and seemed almost to choke on her tears.

"Do you think it was painful death?"

Oh Sally, my Sally. Again I felt so clearly why I loved you. Always putting others before yourself, even when your needs to be consoled were much greater than information about how someone else had suffered.

"We think that's highly unlikely. He had very serious head injuries which would almost certainly have meant instant death. The train had slowed down to about 40 mph, according to the driver, but the mass combined with the speed, well, you can imagine, it must have been nearly instantaneous. My name is Sergeant Richard Mycroft, by the way, Mrs Kent. I'm afraid we need to ask you to come to identify your husband's body soon."

"Of course," Sally replied as the policewoman, whose name was Amy, gave her a cup of tea, which she gratefully held on to.

"Is he, I mean is the person he was still recognisable?"

Sergeant Mycroft looked somewhat relieved at that question.

"Oh yes, it was a blow to the back of his head. His face seems virtually untouched."

Well, well, I thought to myself. I really hadn't taken the trouble to look. I had been so fascinated by the state I was in that I hadn't thought about that. I mean I was obviously dead, so that was that, as far I was concerned.

Amy asked permission to sit down and looked at Sally until she had her attention.

"Mrs Kent, I'm sorry to ask this, but had your husband indicated that he was unhappy or depressed about anything?"

Sally looked at her completely blank for a moment until she understood the implication. It actually made her smile a little. Between her tears and sniffs, she managed to hold onto the smile and say something that showed her intuition was still working at a top rate.

"I suggest you look at the fuel gauge in his van. I'd always had a premonition about something going wrong with his car - his attitude to driving until the final drop of fuel in his tank was left has always made me worry. But suicidal? No, not Geoff. He wasn't really serious enough for that."

Now that made me laugh. That was an entirely new experience and it made my whole being buzz with a similar kind of joy to that which I had felt before in her classroom. In whatever form 'I' was, there was evidently enough awareness to appreciate Sally's humour. It also broke the ice for the police and I felt the atmosphere in the room warm up by a few degrees. A pleasant warmth, not stifling.

"We will certainly do that, Mrs Kent. Would you like Amy to stay with you for a while?"

"That's very kind, but I think I'll be ok. When and where do you want me to come to identify the body?"

They discussed this and various form-filling duties that she had to be a part of and took their leave.

When she was on her own, Sally buried her head in her hands and cried, starting with a howl of protest. A few moments later, she shouted to no-one in particular, apart from me, that is,

"Geoff, you stupid bugger, why didn't you fill up before?"

I knew I was in serious trouble now, she was always very sparing with swearing, and 'bugger' was a word she really only brought out on special occasions.

"I'm sorry, I thought I could get away with it!" I thought to myself.

"Yes, you always do," she responded as if she'd heard me thinking. I saw her shake her head at that moment as if to shake the thought from her brain that she had received some signal from me. She got up and looked in the mirror, as if checking for signs of insanity. Finding nothing but tears and a runny nose, she cleared herself up a bit and made for the phone in her bag and began making the first of probably many calls. The first was to her parents, I left her to it after that and wandered out of the door although I could just have easily have used the window, or a wall. I was becoming more aware of some fascinating capabilities without a living, breathing body.

9.The Funeral

It was odd to be on my own in this different world, but although I felt that help would be at hand when needed, I was enthralled at this new perspective and journey of real self-discovery. My emotions had evidently survived so far, I felt an enormous sadness to have lost Sally as well as the guys with whom I had been making music for over half our lives, particularly after our success and fun at Wacken. We'd all thought of it as a new start, a new career, because it was on a new dimension and dynamic in comparison to what we had reached before.

I didn't really want to leave this world for the next one at all. Who knows, maybe it was a big mistake and 'my time' hadn't come after all? That was already a concept I had never previously thought about and yet it made a kind of sense. There was this feeling of a grid of many dimensions that formed the foundation of life. Life on Earth, maybe life everywhere in the universe. But I was slowly wondering about it. Even on a three dimensional grid, if you happen to go in one direction, other possibilities open themselves up that are on the same grid. So how much more would this apply to a grid that was multi-dimensional? Do we have some kind of infinite choice tempered with certain tendencies to follow laid-out plans? Time was turning out to be relative, as well. Just as the mere thought about Sally had taken me to her, the thought about the accident took me back in time to relive it. It might sound creepy, but it brought an acceptance that was as comforting as reading the final pages of a book to find out what happened at the end of a long plot.

I was able to relive the accident for any number of perspectives that I chose, including from the train driver's seat, which was the worst place to watch the drama unfold. I could also see that, perversely, it had been a kind of choice, although it was shrouded in mist so that I couldn't tell why I would make a choice like that. The chaos was ordered, it wasn't a breakdown of life for me but a continuation of an existence that was beginning to unravel. As time and space had become flexible, I fast-forwarded to my own funeral.

....

The capability of forming a kind of ghost shape was quite easy to grasp, even though I didn't want to be a haunting type of ghost at all. Making myself a very fine 'cosmic costume' from a few surrounding molecules, based on my human shape but completely lacking any sort of density, I sat hovering next to Sally on the front pew in the country chapel. She glanced to her left where I had positioned myself and looked straight at me, presumably seeing nothing. But she let out a long drawn-out sigh which gave me something to connect with. This being all new to me, I was having a hard time interpreting the experience and Sally, the intuitive talent in our relationship, wasn't reacting with signals that made sense to me, either. So we sat there observing preparations before the funeral together, but further apart than we had ever been in over 20 years.

She got up, oblivious to what else was going on around her, and touched the coffin in which my broken body was lying. I hadn't been there to watch her identify my body and although I could probably rewind that incident at will, I currently had no wish to do so. She had removed the gloves she was wearing while she did this and I felt a shudder in my solar-plexus, or the area where it would have been. We were connecting on some level, it seemed to me, even if I hadn't got my head around it so far.

Looking around the chapel, I saw more familiar faces coming in, Mum, Brian, who joined Sally on the front pew, Brian's daughters, their partners and the guys, of course, who also sat close to the front of the church. Death Metallers, finally confronted with the musical niche in which we moved. Patrick's Dad, some clients from my photographic business, even a couple from Jay's office had made it to Alfriston. Geraldine was there, first time I had seen her for ages with a guy in his early twenties. I was moved to see how the place was filling up and noticed the band had brought some guitars and amplifiers as well. This time, I was hoping they wouldn't play that old chestnut, *'Hell has no fury'*.

But I needn't have worried, after the main part of the service Patrick got up and sang, with his most angelic voice, *'Here comes the Sun'*. I did wonder if the congregation knew what it might be in for. True to form, Patrick speeded up and got louder and louder with his growling voice, when he was joined by Jay, Mike and Mary. This was a release for them, I could tell how it was doing them good. The congregation was puzzled to begin with, at least those not familiar with our repertoire, but I saw lots of smiles among the tears.

The line:

'But I say, it's all right!' had them clapping and stamping their feet in a way that wouldn't have been inappropriate in Harlem or Memphis.

'Sun, sun, sun, here it comes
Sun, sun, sun, here it comes
Sun, sun, sun, here it comes'

got everyone joining in, it seemed to me, singing or shouting unrestrained. They even got the timing change right. I wondered if George had funerals in mind when he wrote it. I thought not, probably, but there was nothing more appropriate at that moment for the 70 odd people present. For the first time I was glad I didn't have a body, because people would have seen my emotional hopelessness with enormous tears trickling down my face. As it was I high-fived the guys and my Mum and everyone I felt attached to, which, at that moment was the whole congregation. Goodness knows if they felt anything. Patrick and the guys had created a euphoric moment to make the farewell easier and a positive moment to take home and remember. Sally, in her private grief, was finding it hard to let go completely and I tried to hold her, which is none too easy when you only have a few molecules at your disposal. I was there but absent at the same time. She hugged each band member in turn, obviously grateful for lifting the weight attached to funerals so effectively. Sally lives in a positive world and always has done, even bereavement wouldn't ruin her life, I felt sure of that. Where does she get her positivity from I reflected. Well, it would seem she had vast reservoirs somewhere, she was managing the funeral without neglecting her loss and still able to join in the atmosphere the guys had created.

When you know you are going to be missed, it's like having an honesty mirror placed in front of you in which you can see and feel anything about yourself that you would ever want to know. But the emotions run so high and the love connections are so deep, that the mirror mists over and you can't grasp it for storage to reflect on later. The vicar had said some nice things about me and had also packed in a couple of anecdotes that Sally had obviously provided to take the edge off the event, but awareness for this multi-dimensional grid we were all attached to was such a breathtaking realisation. Sadly, only I had become aware of it, although everyone had been a part of it and still were.

As an experience it wasn't entirely confusing. There was a 'coming home' feeling to everything. We had as a group often joked about death and funerals, and swore to each other that our ashes would be strewn from Birling Gap, one of our favourite places to hang out in the summer. We wanted the ashes to be cast 'into the bosom of the English Channel' which was a line we'd stolen from *'The Big Lebowski',* except that there it had been the Pacific Ocean. Although these had just been jokes and general farting around, I genuinely hoped they would do it and take Sally with them. Even in jokes I recognised a certain reverence and keeping to the script that I believed was in some way valuable. Sally would no doubt rebel first and then relent, once told about our promise to one another. In actual fact, Sally and I were often together at Birling Gap, more than the guys in all probability, so it would be an inclusive experience for her too.

The wake took place at the Cuckmere Inn, not far from Birling Gap as we had often been there for pub lunches and a beer with a view down towards Cuckmere Haven. Patrick and his Dad played some soft Irish music and Mum and Sally sat in a corner in deep conversation with Sally's parents. Here I was again, part of the scene, yet miles away in terms of there being any awareness of my presence. Hard to describe what that presence was. I had detached myself from the molecules I had been using in the chapel, now I was just 'there', an observer without form or function. I did wonder if all souls were present at times like this, on saying goodbye. At that moment, a window of knowledge opened up. I don't know how else to describe it. But as far as I had ever thought about the concept of a soul, which was probably close to never, it had been as a small part of us left over after death. Like a microscopic part of the brain, the heart or something else of significance in the body that lives on, or not. Or maybe from the third eye, behind the forehead, I'd vaguely heard about that too.

Direct knowledge was opening up. Evidently I had asked a significant question, and the answer was explaining itself in what I can only describe as telepathic communication. My understanding was that the essence of a person was a mixture of the role played in a particular life and which parts had chosen to accompany him or her. And the source of where these parts came from could be described as a spirit, much larger in scope and potential than a single life would suggest. Ah, okay, I answered the telepathic source, whatever it was, although it opened up more questions than answers but I didn't want to go there just yet.

10.The Rehearsal

You often hear that expression, 'It's what he would have wanted' in connection with a death's aftermath. How often that makes sense to others, I really couldn't say, but for me when the guys decided that a rehearsal was 'What Geoff would have wanted' only two days after the funeral, I thought,

"Yes, that's right. That is exactly what I want".

So they made their way to Portslade, apart from Mike, who was already there. When Mike closed the shop after lunch on Saturdays it was our chance to start practicing in the back room if we wanted to. My drums were set out as always in the corner. I thought that puzzling to begin with, until I realised they must have taken them from the van and set them up without me. Well of course, how could I have helped? But I saw a certain listlessness in their behaviour, a lack of direction now that one of their number was gone.

"One two, one two," Patrick tested the mic. Jay did some half-hearted tuning of his guitar and Mike played some scales on the keyboard but I saw they were more than likely about to give up. I had to do something quickly to stop them going to the pub for a pointless drink or two. Mike's iPad was on. I discovered you don't need fingers to make a tablet work. Maybe it was tiny electric currents or something, but whatever it was, it was evidently at my disposal. My focus alone was enough to open an app, so I opened Garage Band and started to make some noises until I got the hang of it. It was so quiet I don't think they heard anything, so while I was working out how to get their attention, I tried the intro to '*Hell has no fury*'.

Unusually for hard rock of any sort, let alone Death Metal music, it starts with brushes, then there is a very quick change to thumping bass drum followed by the screaming voice of Patrick at his best. It's a very distinctive intro. When I thought I'd got it about right, I turned up the volume as far as it went and despite the diminutive size of the inbuilt speakers, managed to get heard above the tuning and immediately got their attention. Mike, bless him, was first and his face was turning white when he thought he knew what was going on. Then excitement took over.

"Guys, be quiet for a moment, can you hear that? Or is it me imagining things?" Jay and Patrick joined him, where the iPad was mounted above his keyboard.

They stared at it not believing what their senses were telling them. There was a moment when I thought I would laugh, just to look at their bewildered faces but laughter doesn't have much of an effect without a hollow body in which a sound can reverberate. So I was just watching them looking more and more puzzled as I went through the whole length of *'Fury'*.

When I'd finished Mike removed the iPad and opened a chat programme.

"Geoff is that you? Wtf is going on?" Writing on an electronic keyboard turned out to be child's play.

"Yeah. Just found out how it works and thought I'd join the practice session. Smiley emoji."

They looked at each other in a mixture of excitement and confusion and were at a loss to deal with it.

"Brilliant, mate!"

"So you're still around?"

"Drumming from the grave. Bet that's never been done before!"

"Where are you? Or rather what are you?"

"How does this work?"

"Are you okay?" The last question was really funny, so I answered on the chat programme.

"Well, I am a bit dead, but apart from that I'm fine."

"What does that mean?"

"Don't really know. Except when you're gone, you're not necessarily, if you get my drift."

Pragmatic Mike decided he would take this further and connected the tablet to some powerful bluetooth speakers. I played the intro again.

"Wow, man - that's great!"

He was looking really pleased and it sounded fantastic to my ears, which I no longer had but I could still hear - probably better than before. I noticed that my tinnitus had gone, which may be obvious to some, but I was over the moon as it had adversely affected my hearing. I was most amused that the guys were coming up with a future for the 'Victims' as quickly as I had played my little intro.

"We could take the iPad to gigs!"

"I wonder if people would accept it?"

"This is so cool." And on and on and on.

"So let's go through the whole repertoire," Patrick suggested.

So, possibly for the first time in the history of music, a no longer incarnate musician played live with his band members their current repertoire of Death Metal numbers. I did wonder whether Natalie's Cole's duet with her father from the grave would count as music with a discarnate (is that even a word?) but it wasn't live, and this was. So we were making history although the discussion was already taking place about whether this would be accepted by our fans.

"Guys, I may not always be available. You need to think about that. At some point this connection is presumably going to end," I chatted back.

"Also, it may not go down very well. It is kind of morbid for a Death metal band to have a dead member."

"We can always say it's a recording," Mike suggested. Jay and Patrick went along with that idea and discussed the next gig. It wasn't going to be far away, nor was it a big venue, so they asked if I'd like to try it out.

"Sure. I'm not going anywhere."

11.First Gig

So the guys decided to try it out on their next visit to a pub with a stage, in Haywards Heath. They were very concerned and had every right to be. Autumn was beginning and people were staying inside pubs now, rather than heading straight for the beer garden. This was a place we had played before, even when we were just a cover band without Patrick so we had quite a history with them, going back almost 25 years. Mike wasn't sure whether they should set the drums up on stage, or just the iPad and speakers. There was much discussion about how to sell the drummer's absence/presence paradox to the public. Patrick, who I had seen crossing himself when we had been chatting, was in favour of coming clean up to a point, leaving the drum kit at home and saying we had top quality recordings of the drumming for our whole repertoire which I had apparently left for them to find 'in case something happened'. This idea was the one the guys decided to go with and went ahead.

Although I was freely using my recent discovery about the nature of time and its flexibility, I decided to stay in Earth time and share their anticipation. I also realised I was going to have to play as well as I ever had, in these somewhat odd conditions and my nervousness was a connection to an emotion I hadn't felt since struggling with the van at the rail crossing.

"Good evening to you all, fans of Valhalla Victims, the world's smallest 4-piece Death Metal band!"

Patrick was in top form, so much was obvious and the crowd was taking notice, always a challenge when you play in pubs and compete with beer, wine and high spirits. Most were evidently aware of my death and there was quite a push to get to the front of the stage and share in the curiosity.

He took the mic off the stand and looked around the room.

"As many of you know, we are still in shock at the sudden loss of our drummer, Geoff Kent, who died in an accident not too far from here."

There were grunts and claps and general murmurs from those who seemed to have been in the know. More came into the room, which would probably hold about 150 people and it was filling up rapidly.

"When someone dies, there is often a contemplative moment of silence, maybe a minute or so. But we aren't into silence so much. Noise is our thing."

A couple of approving shouts came up from the room and the mood was one of approval.

"Yeah, bring it on, Victims!"

Several other shouts and the double vee sign pointing upwards came in waves from the back of the room to the stage. Patrick looked towards Jay and Mike and saw they were both grinning and revelling in the moment. He gave them a conspiratorial wink and turning his attention back to the crowd, he offered an explanation.

"So we found some files we hadn't known about. It seems our drummer, Geoff Kent, was planning something and had made recordings of our complete repertoire, probably only a few weeks before his accident. Hence the speakers and no drums on stage. So we'll still be playing with him in spirit!"

Yes, I thought. That's about as close as he could dare to be. He stepped back from the mic and moved his guitar around to its playing position, with the shout,

"Let's go!"

My signal for the brushes, followed by the cymbal crash and bass drum pounding, and the crowd evidently knew our music. They started screaming and jumping around in anticipation as Patrick approached the mic with the first lines of *'Hell has no fury'*.

We had never, ever had a gig that was quite as electric. The joint was rocking and rolling and the size was about right to make it work well. I watched it all from above, hovering around ceiling height - it was amazing to see this group of people move and groove as if one whole unit was working in ecstatic harmony. Fascinating. It was then I noticed that I was in two places at once, concentrating on the drumming app and watching the gig from above at the same time. I was still learning about being dead, and probably breaking protocol, but my explanation for the two places at once was related to the elasticity of time in relation to space and personhood, if that's a word. How odd, but how exciting. I must tell the guys about it later.

They were having the time of their lives too. I could see drops of sweat falling from Mike's forehead onto the keyboard as he skidded across the keys with a speed and excitement in his fingers. It was riveting to look at and I recognised similar energy sparks interacting with him as those I saw at Sally's class the day I died. Some awareness of mine dipped down into the notes and watched them become images, cosmic in their appearance. I was experiencing another dimension, but it wasn't quite the night sky I was looking at. Multi-coloured circular vibrations would follow each other, apparently miles apart and slip in and out of connection in an unbelievable rush of depth and void, becoming meteorite like lumps when he hit a disharmony, explosions from above and below in colours that I couldn't describe, it was like witnessing a Big Bang. My perception was being stretched at each moment and I began to see how the band was working together, with Jay's guitar building coastlines above and within the whole picture, then forming mountains, valleys, oceans, deserts that disappeared as quickly as they arrived. My drumming was framing the images with squares, see-though cubes tumbling though space, pyramids and other shapes the names of which I don't know. Patrick was producing spaceships and satellites with his lead guitar that often appeared to narrowly avoiding crashing into one another. And then his voice! It produced colour changes in the background, flowing in waves and crashing on the surf of Jay's landscapes. This was quite a trip. I saw that my awareness was everywhere, I wasn't potentially limited to one or two places, this was number four at least and I could see there were plenty more pockets of consciousness I could have explored at the same moment.

In the break for applause towards the end, I was wondering if what I had been watching were dreamworlds that I had generated with the help of the music. They were extremely realistic and left me with the sense that realism needed to be redefined. At least in my mind. I had left myself with a lot to think about. Or maybe I'd left myself with a lot to dream about. Whichever way it was, my existence was proving to offer more depth and discovery than I could have imagined.

....

Patrick's Dad was helping put the gear in my undamaged van and cornered his son.

"Patrick, what was that all about? It was a great gig, I can see that, but how come you didn't tell me about Geoff leaving those drumming files?"

"Because we didn't know how it would go down. We've only had a couple of rehearsals with them and it was a bit of luck that we found them anyway."

Jack was willing to go along with that.

"But I tell you, it sounded as live as ever. More so, maybe. Geoff must have prepared that really well."

"I think he must have done, Dad. Maybe he had some kind of premonition that they'd be needed some day."

Jay slapped Patrick on the back and handed him a heavy roll of cable to carry out to the van with Mike and our helpers. We were always a hands-on team and Jack's road management was great, but he did rely on some help from us as well, as you never knew how many volunteers would turn up to give us a hand.

It was a clear night and Jack was on his own, a short distance from the van, looking up to the night sky. He seemed to be struggling with his own thoughts and memories.

While Jay and Mike were struggling to manoeuvre an amplifier into the back of the van, Patrick leaned against the rear of the open vehicle and spoke, almost to himself but he was okay that the other two were still around to hear.

"So where is Geoff now? Is he sitting on some cloud playing a harp looking down at us and joining in the fun when he feels like it? Or is he listening in right now, aware of our thoughts and conversations? I don't know about you guys, but I find it quite creepy. And fun, yes. I mean he played better than ever tonight, he didn't miss a beat! I usually do stuff that I understand and this is way off my horizon!"

"Get your phone out and ask him!" Jay suggested. That earned him a wry smile from Patrick.

"You know I hadn't thought of that. I'll send him an email."

"Cool, good idea." Mike sat down next to Patrick and Jay stood next to him, peering over his shoulder as Patrick began typing.

"Hi, Geoff. How did you enjoy it tonight?"

Patrick wanted to write to my old address. But there wasn't much point in that, so I just used use Patrick's keyboard and I saw the guys watch in fascination as I typed my answer, gasping at every letter. As well as the speed I was writing in.

"Loved it, absolutely loved it. Saw it from all sorts of angles too. Bit difficult to explain but it was a multi-media event for me."

"Wha?"

My reply was a row of faces with the emoji of crying with laughter. Saw them laugh and wipe some tears from their eyes at that answer.

"So wtf are you and where are you?"

"I don't know. I don't think you're supposed to hang around the planet once you're dead. Not that I'm a ghost, but I just seem to have some unfinished business. With the band, with Sally, maybe my Mum. I don't know where I am exactly as tonight I discovered I could be in more than one place at one time."

Mike wanted to write, but as he said it anyway, I didn't need to read it.

"What, like quantum physics? Being in more than one place at one time?"

"Maybe it is like that, I couldn't say. But since the accident, I have experienced so much stuff I can only describe as multi-dimensional."

"So have you met anyone else?" Patrick again.

"No I haven't, although I'm kind of aware of a close presence which feels like personal energy. Also, at the moment you said that, a timeless image - not a bit like the old lady she was when she died - but a kind of 3-d image of my grandma appeared briefly in front of my eyes. Which I no longer have, of course. But the senses don't need the organs apparently."

"This is crazy stuff," Jay said, grabbing the phone.

"You don't need it Jay, he can hear you anyway." Mike handed it back to Patrick.

"Well no-one was more surprised than I was after that train hit me. After the brief pain I was in a good place. It felt like home in some ways. But it was also a new, original experience. I'm still working it out."

"Okay, but that was a while ago now. What have you been doing in the meantime?"

"I think time is a bit like a jukebox. You can choose the next significant event from a choice of many. Not that it looks like one of those old-fashioned jukeboxes at all, but it's the only metaphor I can think of right now. So, you choose your event, or place or person and it plays out for you. Time is flexible, it can stretch out or become compressed, whatever you happen to focus on."

"Well I don't think I'll try explaining that to my Dad!" Patrick snapped his phone shut and made for the back entrance of the pub. Jay and Mike looked at each other, shrugged and followed him. They continued to grab the remaining gear and pack it into the van while

Patrick was sitting in a corner with his dad, who was cradling a half-pint of beer.

"Hey, can we talk?"

"Sure Patrick, why not."

"Da, you know this Death Metal business was all Geoff's idea?"

"Yes, I remember that."

"Well, he was concerned that we might break up or there might be a change in line-up, he mentioned that to me."

"So?"

"I think he wanted to preserve a legacy or something. He recorded all our stuff to have something that he would remember. Like a kind of insurance policy against forgetting. He didn't talk to us about it, I think it was quite personal. But it did make a kind of sense when we found the files."

As it happens, some files did exist as well. Mike had meticulously recorded the drum rehearsals. Not quite a live performance, but Mike had mixed them up a bit to generate the best version he could. They could certainly be a fall-back option if I wasn't around to pay digital drums.

12.Sally

The worst and the best thing about being dead was not having a body to deal with. The lightness of being was astonishing and it is a freeing up from density that is a joy to experience. I could think, I could see, I could smell, I could hear, but I couldn't taste and I couldn't touch. I could remember taste and touch, but it wasn't quite the same and I understood, probably for the first time, how creative touch is and essential to the life experience.

I wanted to touch Sally. I wanted to kiss her, taste those kisses, hold her, bury my face in her, feel the shape of her that I have loved for so long and touch the lids of those blue eyes and stroke the Snow White dark hair that stopped just short of her shoulders. I wanted to go for long walks in her blue eyes, those sad but bright lights of her spirit. My vocabulary was changing too, I was using terms that I avoided in my living life as I couldn't define them well at all. I couldn't define the terms now either, but their presence needed recognition. Sally was an avid reader and wouldn't steer clear of any subject, no matter how unfamiliar she felt she was with it. Basically, I think she had a desire to understand everything. And everyone, come to that. As a result, she read all sorts of esoteric stuff and would have known much more naturally than I did what to call these features of life/death.

These thoughts sent me floating to our back garden, where I found her tending some plants. She had planted courgettes, beetroot, potatoes, beans and a whole lot of other vegetables that I wasn't very good at naming. Yes, I knew we had lettuce, but wasn't sure what kind, ditto tomatoes. She had even successfully produced peppers one summer, but I don't think the plants had flourished this summer. But for Sally, the garden was a place of solace, regeneration. I admired her for it, but couldn't join in as a whole-hearted paid-up member of an enthusiastic garden community.

It was no surprise to find her harvesting some courgettes and thinning her row of lettuces next to them. Would I be invading her privacy to talk to her? Surely not, we've been partners for a long time. How best to grab her attention? Phone apps were the easiest way so far and her phone was on our bench. I thought about that last connection to the guys and the next moment I was zipped backed to our rehearsal room in Portslade. It was quiet, the store was open but no-one was rehearsing or trying out a new instrument or other gadget so I sat down on my drum stool. Obviously, without a body there was no need for a seat, but it was a source of comfort and had the familiarity that I needed right now. It also had form, having used quiet moments like this in the past to think straight. If I am actually present in the garden, even though she'd be unable to see me, the shock might be too much for her. I worked out it would be better to approach from a distance. Where to begin?

I began to visit some of our old haunts. I found there wasn't a huge difference in imagining these places in my mind and actually going there, the memory itself was enough to take me there in a highly realistic manner, even though I noticed it was a rerun of a previous experience that was significant. The beach at Birling Gap. We had met there after Sally's examination at the gynaecologist. It was bad news insofar as the chance of becoming a mother was slim, to say the least. But in Sally's mind there is always good news behind the bad.

"We can make love with true abandon, Geoff. No messy condoms or those horrid pills anymore!"

I thought our lovemaking was always pretty much with true abandon, but I understood what she meant. As well as the fact that we hadn't used any birth control methods for quite a few months now, in the hope of pregnancy. Sally has a resistance to negativity that probably is the reason she is such a wonderful and popular teacher with her disabled children. I saw the scene as an observer, not from my own perspective, but as someone watching. There was a reason why we didn't have children. The higher intention was precisely because of Sally's devotion to her disabled kids. She had agreed to the decision with herself. Now that was a strange message. I realised it meant with her 'higher self', to enable her essence to stay focused on the many children who needed her. Sally is a remarkable person who loves helping people - as well as myself on the night we first met.

The concept of the grid came back into view. Not a fork in the road but many alternatives present themselves in our lives and that is what makes our Earth so special, as we live on one of those rare planets whose inhabitants have free will.

Really? This was weird, but I was also beginning to understand that it was part of Sally's private beliefs that I was now privy to. Why she regularly practiced yoga maybe as well. Just after the start of the millennium, I was taking pictures for an internet provider on location in Antibes in the South of France, creating a digital world on a car park that was a kind of a covered asphalt peninsula from which you would only see the Mediterranean beyond, if you found the right position. We had agreed to meet up after the job and spend a week or so on holiday. We had a cool hotel to stay in and it was quite one of the most memorable holidays we'd ever had. But whether at the pool or the beach, if we were just relaxing, Sally had her current book with her - 'The Tibetan book of the Dead'.

"Isn't that a bit morbid, love? Specially as holiday reading." I asked her after I'd picked her up at Nice airport and it was lying there exposed, on top of her shopping bag.

"No, not really. It's not morbid so much as an insight into life itself, by understanding the process of death. Anyway, isn't that a bit rich, coming from a Death Metal drummer?"

We both had to laugh at that, my hypocrisy was a bit too obvious. She gave me one of her innocent smiles as we sped along the Promenade des Anglais, marvelling at the top weather conditions and looking forward to some quality time together. This kind of experience was lost as a physical entity, but it was a memory that became clearer now than while I was still alive. I found myself laughing and smiling just the same way as I had then, emotionally it was a perfect fit.

It was then that I had the idea that I thought might work and be the best way to get in contact to Sally in a more subtle way.

....

I chose a moment when she was listening to music. She had a speaker on in the kitchen, while she was chopping parsley and celery sticks. Her playlist was set to random ballads, from the 60s to the 90s. Having mostly played heavy and hard, you might think that was all I was interested in, but actually we enjoyed singing along to all sorts of things. And my Mum's devotion to 60s music had made quite an expert out of me.

I sorted through the list and found *Unchained Melody* by the Righteous Brothers and set it to come up next. It was our joke song, although we both loved it, but I often made suggestive remarks about Sally taking up pottery so that I could fondle her from behind, repeating the scene from the film *'Ghost'*. She usually replied that we didn't need to watch it for me to grab her from behind, but it was always a convenient excuse for me to do so. We had often seen it and I felt embarrassed that it was our favourite so we didn't tell another soul. Least of all the Victims! But Mum always played 60s music and I think we both felt there was something profound about those years.

The song came on and Sally stared at the speaker first, in apparent disbelief. A tear or two welled up in her eyes. Then she grabbed 5 or 6 sticks of celery and formed them into the shape of a tower, holding them at the bottom, as if clutching clay to form a jug. She was playing Demi Moore and I would have been Patrick Swayze. It was such a sentimental scene in the movie and we'd both been brought up with a refusal to accept sentimentality as a virtue, yet it often grabbed us quite emotionally when we saw extracts on youtube or repeats on tv. I couldn't have told the guys, and here I was choosing a recording from beyond the grave. Not Metallica or Led Zeppelin, but the Righteous Brothers.

'I've hungered for your touch', I was feeling that more than I had ever felt before.

So I tried to embrace her from behind and saw her body shiver, even though I didn't have a presence or anything you could reasonably describe as a body. Sally 'danced' with me while the music played and if I'd had cheeks, they would have had tears running down them like Sally's. It was a release for Sally and a release for me, to be alone together in these strange circumstances. Joined in our love, it hadn't left us yet. As the falsetto voice rose to,

'I need your love' Sally stopped dancing, balancing herself at the kitchen work surface, she wiped her hands on a paper towel and picked up her mobile phone and opened Notes.

She then simply wrote,

"Where are you Geoff?"

I answered:

"Right here."

"I thought so. You put that track on, didn't you?"

"Yes, I thought you'd know I was around."

"I did indeed. Quite quickly in fact. So, what is it like to be dead? Obviously not quite what you expected?"

"No, probably closer to what you expected. But I am not a ghost and have no desire to become one. For some reason, I'm still around though. I can see there are other worlds available but right now I'm not exactly stuck, but feel I have some loose ends to fix."

She picked up her phone and walked over to the couch to sit down and absorb what was going on. I realised that she didn't need to use an app, as I understood the next question before she had time to write it out.

"What do you need to do?"

"I don't know exactly what I should do, but doors open, so to speak and I walk into rooms and something happens, more or less of its own accord."

"Hey, you can read my mi…"

"Only because we are having a conversation. It's just like talking to each other. You say something and I respond. I can't and wouldn't read your mind if we weren't talking to one another."

"So the ground rules are similar in a way. I'm receiving every word - just as if you were speaking."

"Yes, in some ways nothing much has changed. But the scope is wider and deeper than when you're alive. With the exception, of course, that you no longer have a body."

"But you still have a presence. I feel it quite strongly."

"Maybe that's because you are sensitive to things of that nature." Sally giggled at that remark.

"That doesn't sound like the Geoff I know! 'Sensitive to things of that nature!' You'd have laughed at me if I had said something like that!"

"Yes, I suppose I've changed quite a lot. But I'm more me than I ever have been before, if you know what I mean."

By this time we had both become pretty good at telepathy. I was hearing or sensing her questions and she was sensing my answers. She didn't seem particularly fazed by all this. And it wasn't just the sense or emotion that we were sending to each other. Exactly like in a normal conversation, we were understanding each word.

"I think I do, Geoff. Your essence is unfiltered, perhaps with the added depth you spoke about. What's the best thing about not having a body?"

"I have a feeling of lightness, which I suppose is no surprise. But I seem to be able to trigger any memory, any time , any place and I can revisit them as a spectator to events I have experienced before. Or as a participant, it feels quite limitless in scope. Space and time are so malleable here, you can manipulate things to be a rerun, even with a different outcome."

"Whoa! So how does that work?"

"It's like a projection of what would have happened if I had taken another route. But the other route looks real too, so it's quite a challenge to decide on what the real world really is in a physical and mental context."

"And the accident could have had another outcome too?"

This question sent me straight back to the scene at the level crossing. It was a perfectly orderly scene with me waiting in the van, first in line at the crossing. I looked at the fuel gauge and saw that I had plenty left and 'remembered' I had stopped in Pyecombe to fill up. Everything else looked the same. The train approached and drove through without incident. The barriers went up and a motorcyclist was overtaking a car with two elderly ladies inside, who were taking their time to restart. He missed me by a couple of inches because I braked while I was still on the tracks, allowing him enough space to pass by without causing damage to himself or to me. Was it energy, 'something in the air' that I felt? It could have been that way, it was evident. Apparently things aren't pre-ordained but had a likelihood scale, for want of a better description.

For the first time, thoughts of choice came into mind. No, I hadn't chosen to have my brains blown out by a regional train, but I had made a choice of experience, long, long ago, before my birth, to share my experience with some of my closest friends. And they had been in on the deal in a manner of speaking. I had volunteered to be some kind of messenger and share with close friends our common destiny. I saw my friends in their spirit images, instantly recognisable, and Sally was part of the whole deal, a messenger herself on numerous occasions. Which suggested we had all been here before, had lived and died many times over. In life, when Sally had wanted to talk to me about reincarnation, I had rejected the idea and found it to be a morbid idea too, like reading the "Tibetan Book of the Dead" on holiday. Which apparently has numerous references to finding a suitable new body after death, but I had asked her to keep it to herself.

"This one life is plenty enough for me to cope with, thank you very much," was my usual retort. She never insisted and we left it unanswered, hanging in the air between us. Also I never had much time for religion, whereas Sally wasn't afraid to read any book she felt attracted to and religious books featured quite strongly, as they were often the only ones which entered that area, mostly those concerning eastern religion. Then there was alternative psychology, which she got into later. It would be wrong to say Sally didn't care that I had died, but she had a willingness to go with the flow of winds of change and fate, and I believe it gave her a lot of strength. She missed me enormously and we were still connected through our love, which hadn't lost its power in the least. But the connection we had discovered after my death had a depth which was surely a huge comfort.

After this reenactment at the crossing I found my connection to Sally had been interrupted and I was floating away, towards the coast and upwards towards the afternoon sky.

13. Memory Bank

Gliding through the afternoon sky, I came to a scene that was unfolding in front of me. A typical Sussex village was in my line of vision, a narrow street with bunting hanging from the roofs of two stone cottages.

'Welcome to Valhalla, Geoff!' it read in large letters. It was just hanging there, in the afternoon sky, as physical as if it had just been hung up a few moments previously. I got in really close to examine the details and then it was obvious that it was more a projection, a kind of holographic image. Was it my own mind doing the projecting?

I can't say how I had imagined life after death to be, but a Sussex village decorated with bunting would not have been my first guess. There was evidently the Geoff who had been alive for 47 years on Earth, and I was coming to some kind of a reception that was so realistic that it was hard to separate from the so-called real world. Beyond the entrance to the village, I saw more buildings that looked familiar, at least in style, although not a place I specifically recognised. I found I could walk along the pavement and here I was, on my own in a fantasy world that still had a vague sense of familiarity for me.

I walked past a post office and newsagent, a tearoom, a hotel, a supermarket and a laundromat, none of which would have looked out of place in Uckfield or Hurstpierpoint. A pub in the distance caught my eye and it felt like it was my destination, as they often had been in life. The painted sign above the entrance was too far away to read, but as I got closer, it became much clearer and I was able to read the pub name: 'The Memory Bank'. The entrance was open ("Would I have been able to walk through a closed door?" I reflected) as I walked in. Every feature so far was not unusual, almost designed to make me feel relaxed in an unthreatening setting.

Walking inside was a thoroughly comforting experience. A bar with apparently a good choice of beers, some cider on tap as well, and much of the paraphernalia associated with an average British pub. Upturned spirit bottles mounted on the wall, two fridges filled with wine bottles, an electronic one-armed bandit, a darts corner. But it was empty, as far as I could tell. So I sat down, wondering what would happen next. Evidently I wasn't in control of this experience, so there was no point in trying to project ideas or images into the scene in front of me. I would wait and see what happened next.

"Sorry to keep you waiting sir! What would you like?" A barman had just entered the bar and was wiping his hands on a small towel attached to his belt.

"Well, I'd love a pint of bitter," I replied, feeling a bit ridiculous that he could supply me with one. But he pulled an excellent pint glass for me and I came closer to the bar and sat on a stool. He looked at me with an amused expression while he passed the beer glass across the bar. I knew his face from somewhere but for a moment I couldn't place it. I would have placed him in his early 30s and it took me a moment to imagine him in uniform and then it dawned on me. He looked like John. The grandpa I had never met. I didn't know what to say.

The amusement in his eyes was still there.

"How do you like our beer sir?" Dumbfounded at what was happening, I decided I'd grab the glass and try to drink it. Without a body of flesh and blood, you'd think there'd be no point in trying, but in actual fact although I couldn't drink in that sense, the experience was so similar that I was for a moment thinking maybe I hadn't yet left the Earth. The wonderful essence of the beer was absolutely available to me, despite my lack of body parts.

"It's very nice, thank you!" My British awkwardness, or fear of embarrassment was keeping me polite and reserved, evidently much to the amusement of the landlord. Placing an elbow on the bar, he leaned over towards me in that intimate way of landlords everywhere, when they think no-one else can eavesdrop.

"How do you like the Memory Bank so far?"

"It's wonderful. Also a bit confusing. But you look a lot like my grandfather."

"Well that's because I was your grandfather last time around, although we never met. Pleased to meet you, Geoff!" Saying we then shook hands would be a grossly misleading description of what happened. I would describe it more as a meeting of energies and a sparkling multi-media event. He showered sparks and rainbow colours around his body on making contact with mine. His energy was full of humour and expectation, it made its way to the core of my consciousness with a direct hit, waking me up to still other forms of experience.

"Let me show you." He came out from behind the bar and walked over to the one-armed bandit.

'Grandpa' John began hitting the buttons to make the images whirl, as I watched in fascination as they produced rather different results than I had anticipated. When the three dials came to a standstill, a sphere of a scene popped out of the machine. To begin with, it was a little like a snow globe, born out of the final moment of standstill. Then more came out of the machine, like soap bubbles and when I began to focus on a particular bubble, it grew larger and show recognisable features. In fact, it was such that they were like miniature theatre stages, with various participants coming visibly into focus. Inside one bubble I saw myself carefully loading my newly-repaired drum set into the van and getting into the driver's seat. By this time the size was growing so rapidly, that it was reaching realistic dimensions.

"Pyecombe was a chance, but the whole group who were in on this were in agreement that the level crossing was the ideal solution. Even the train driver who you don't even know was in agreement." John was looking at me with a wise expression.

"Not everything happens for a reason, but key issues generally do."

I was fascinated in following this reenactment. The intricate details, even the weather and general atmosphere were such accurate depictions of that fateful day.

"The whole world's a stage" I said quoting Shakespeare's 'As you like it'.

" 'And all the men and women merely players; They have their exits and their entrances, And one man in his time plays many parts.' Exactly," John smiled. "Shakespeare knew a thing or two."

We had studied the play at school in the 5th form, but I hadn't thought of it then as having had some kind of deeper meaning than a simple metaphor for our lives.

"Why do we need stages to play out our lives, John?" By this time, I felt I could safely leave out the prefix 'Grandpa'. He looked as if he was younger than me.

"It's just drama, Geoff. As long as there is drama in our lives we learn from the experience. If learning was only from books and teachers, we would lack experience. "

"So you are saying that I was actor and director of the story of my life's ending?" I was unsure if this is what it meant but it did seem to fit the logic of our conversation.

"Yes, in a way. You and other travellers on the same road. And not just the end but the many stages of your life which were of importance. Life offers many stages, both in the sense of time and platforms. Each one of significance moves you to the next level of learning and experience."

"Why do we need this kind of learning? Why can't we learn from books or these projections?"

"You can and you do. However, there is nothing quite comparable to an experience lived through on Earth. Relationships which are all love and light here can become violent or at the very least dysfunctional on Earth. We need the drama to work things out so in a future life we can mine the vein of experience we have been through. Only then will we have integrated this attitude into our essence. Some issues take several lives before this is achieved. Moving towards an all-embracing love of 'beinghood'. Between lives we know that this is true. On the Earth we forget, mainly by the time we are 7 years old at the latest. Many children still remember when they are very young, but are not given the means to express their memories. By the time they would be able to, they have forgotten. Apart from their sensibility to life which has settled itself into their being as the result of previous experiences. We remain in largely well-defined groups, although there is no limit on Earth to whoever else we decide to come into contact with."

"Well," I started a small complaint,"It must have made sense to someone when this whole 'life' thing began."

John gave me a look of wisdom and amusement.

"You do know we are each of us responsible for this 'life thing', as you call it? There is no higher being who orders us to behave in a certain way. We have chosen this way for a reason and free will is a vital part of it. It is an open method, if you like. The outcome is uncertain, creative, multi-dimensional, it is whatever you want to make of it. There is no crime or punishment as everything is experience and both right and wrong in your terms are possible. Our universe allows bad things to happen and good things frequently come out of so-called bad things. Lessons are learned best when they are more dramatic."

Although my memory was returning, integrating much of what he was telling me was still a lot of effort. My mind was apparently still in the context of life on Earth. We were now sitting in the beer garden which felt so real, it was even harder to relate to another dimension. But I didn't want to stop John from his explanation.

"Sally has a long history of understanding other forms of consciousness, which is why she volunteered to take the hardest role in the whole drama. Her strength of character helps her overcome grief and suffering better than most. She has been a guide and messenger many times and for that reason she passionately enjoys the role of helping others. Her default setting is love, as you were able to appreciate."

"I did indeed." I felt sadness and love for Sally overcoming me. So I changed the subject.

"But despite all my own issues, what about the dreadful state the world is in right now? It doesn't seem intelligent or reasonable to allow that stuff to happen. The wars since the beginning of the new millennium, hunger, extreme weather, climate change, refugees, pollution, I could go on."

"Of course you could. Theoretically, all the hardship from the world could be removed at the cosmic blink of an eye. But that would mean breaking the highest law in place which partners free will, which is non-interference."

"But we are a race apparently determined to destroy our own future and that of the planet. Surely there is a limit to how much 'non-interference' is acceptable?"

"Indeed. We are working on it now and have been for a while. Memories are less closed off from their true roots than they used to be. People are slowly remembering things. Children remember for longer where they come from and are beginning to tell their parents. There have never been as many messengers - like yourself - working out the dramas for others to learn. Sally has been a powerful tool for change in many lives, she's often been there to guide you, even when you haven't had a personal relationship like this time around.

"Dreams are being experienced in a more meaningful way than in previous ages. People don't filter dreams and this allows them to consider other ideas and forms that had previously seemed unthinkable. It takes time to absorb these issues into their system, but in terms of consciousness they are already there for many people and will find their way to the surface in due course."

While I recognised the truth of what John was telling me, I was still shocked at the ineptitude of political leaders and the damage that was being done in the meantime. He caught my thoughts and countered,

"The Earth will never be a perfect place. That's not its purpose. It is a playground, a learning facility, even a correcting facility. All sorts of things are available for experiment and discovery. Mankind needs the imperfect to strive for more and there are plenty of roads to choose from. Nothing is lost as every experience can be examined and reexamined between lives when the cosmic memory bank reopens. Earth itself allows for experience and will show us that every life is limited, whereas what you term death has no limits. Everything is valuable, although little is real in the true sense of the word. Your memory is returning to you slowly, so as not to overwhelm you with its power."

"So what is really real?" I asked and the answer came to me at the same moment as his reply.

"Only love."

14.Only Love

Thoughts of love sent me back to Sally's kitchen, without loss of time.

"And the accident could have had another outcome too?"

"Yes, but it was what a number of us agreed to, it seems to me."

"What an odd thing to agree to."

"I know. We are here to learn in so many different ways and it's hard to see why things would happen if we don't share the bigger picture. But it's like pieces of an intricate puzzle that do actually fit together. In our lives, you knew much more about this stuff than I did."

Sally looked straight at me, which was a strange and wonderful feeling as in most senses of the word I wasn't there at all.

"What are you now, Geoff? I mean in terms of energy, do you have a body of any sort, or dimensions?"

"I don't know. I definitely have a body on the other side, so to speak. An energy body, if you like. It can morph and change at will, but when I'm back on Earth, it's hard to say what I am, exactly. Awareness, certainly. Not confined to a shape. Maybe it's easiest to imagine a tiny dot of light?"

Sally smiled at this.

"That's about what I thought! You're obviously not physically here, but your awareness is present. When you first started chatting with me on the phone, you were using your light awareness to manipulate the letters on my keyboard. I felt that quite strongly, until we started communicating telepathically."

"Travel is virtually instant in this form. I've been on both sides of this awareness without the need to cross a border. I was away for quite a while talking to my guide, yet no time passed on Earth."

"I want to hold you, Geoff!" I saw tears well up in her eyes and felt I would do the same if I could.

"Look out for me in your dreams," I suggested. I knew Sally had been interested in dreams and lucid dreaming and she looked pleased with the idea.

So this was to be my first outing as a lucid dreamer.

15.Lucid Dreaming

Not having a body, I didn't need to sleep, of course, and waiting for Sally to begin rapid eye movement sleep didn't take more than a blink. It was so cool to see her calmly leave her body in this state, but still looking like the Sally I know and love. Now I had a body too, like the one that I had had when talking to John. I knew the body's shape could change, but for Sally I wanted to be as close as possible to the Geoff she knows.

She seemed to be in her own world to begin with, floating around our bedroom then beyond to her beloved garden. The crops and flowers in her garden evidently required her attention and they were shining in apparent anticipation. In an embrace of their energy to Sally's, I saw an exchange of lovingness flow from between them, pulsating in a multicoloured vibration, a proper light show. The energy seemed to be connecting outwards into the dark sky.

"I wanted to show you that," she told me as she continued this process. I couldn't help smiling at her casualness at communicating with me in a dream, while her waking self still had filters and didn't allow for the kind of openness that was apparently natural in dreams.

"I'm impressed," I said, "but I thought you wanted an embrace?"

"Oh, we'll come to that soon enough," Sally laughed in my face. "Let's look at what else the garden has to offer first."

I was coming to understand that although I could have virtually any question answered in this state, it was up to me to ask the right questions. And Sally was way ahead of me in so many ways.

One area of our garden always seemed to thrive better than others and Sally showed me how two broad lines of a grid of sparkling energy met at that point in the garden. A couple of square meters of increased energy was enough to allow all the plants to reach their potential. We had harvested some impressive cauliflowers, beans, tomatoes, sunflowers. Sally called the space her 'Little Findhorn'. Yet as far as I know, in her normal waking state, Sally didn't know much about energy lines.

Reading my thoughts, she spoke to me again.

"That's right, I don't know too much about it, but enough to suspect that something is happening. In my dream state I can see things quite clearly and I leave clues for my waking state, such as turning a sunflower away from the sun but still showing me its full beauty when I walk into the garden."

I went over to the bench under our apple tree and sat down, so as to be in a position I was familiar with. Sally joined me and held my hand.

"The dream state is so real," I told her. "It's almost confusing to consider it, knowing how real we consider our daily lives to be."

"I'll let you be in my dreams if I can be in yours!"

Sally laughed and her perfect smile reminded me of our physical life, which came with a sense of yearning for a physical touch, which Sally felt too.

"Physical touch is exciting because of energy transfer," and with that thought she embraced me with a passion that was as keen a reminder of our loving as I could imagine.

"So what do you remember in this state?" I asked her.

"Well, most things that are crucial in our lives have been acted out or reenacted in this state including your accident, so potentially, we have a clue about everything of significance. My physical filters only allow hints of what we rehearse to work their way through to my waking consciousness, but owing to repetition and dream memory, it is usually enough to remove the sharpest sting from the scariest moments. I was at school when the accident happened, and I felt a jump in my consciousness, a frightening dread, which was rapidly followed by a feeling of reassurance."

"Whoa. Hard to process all the same, isn't it?"

"Yes, it's not easy, but it's for a purpose that we all worked on. A guiding hand provided me with a strength I didn't feel, yet knew I had access to. Am I making sense to you?"

"I think so. My grandpa John has given me some clues too. Apparently it's unusual to hang around the Earth as I'm doing, but something keeps me here for longer and with more direct communication than most can take part in. You seem to be a special agent, a frequent messenger and insider."

Sally looked up to the skies and stretched her dream body.

"Sometimes I recall episodes from another existence and they come to me as real as our current moment. I don't know how to look at them objectively, but I do get a feeling for the present moment in each context and this life feels similar in many ways."

"You should be promoted and become a spirit guide!" I meant it seriously and I saw her face change to an expression of wisdom.

"I love this planet and its inhabitants. I want to be a part of life here as often as I can. In some ways, everything makes sense and when you know that, even if it is only vague knowledge or memory, it can sustain you through anything life throws at you."

"Which is why you weren't fazed by the young man reading '1984' on New Year's Eve, I guess."

"That's right. The book was to be our signal, and although I didn't recognise that particular fact, the emotional coming together was so strong, that I felt that destiny was opening a new chapter."

Sally's certainty had always been her strength. I felt quite ungifted in that respect. I was just a reasonable drummer and an enthusiastic photographer, but hadn't shared her spiritual gifts at all. I avoided them if I could, feeling sceptical at least, or maybe just out of my depth. Again, she was following my thought patterns.

"Geoff, you have had all sorts of different lives. You had four consecutive lives just to learn humility and then you needed to relearn leadership because you'd become too humble! But every life has its purpose and none are without value, on this planet or beyond."

A kind of predawn change in the light was a signal for Sally to return to her sleeping body. We embraced again with the power we'd felt before, even more intense this time around. I watched her form drift back through the house into our bedroom, leaving me with the plants and dreamscape of our garden. It was obviously real, but differently real, governed by a completely other set of rules.

This connection with Sally gave me a lot of strength and satisfaction, tinged though it was with sadness too. I knew this was a kind of exceptional treat, and would come to an end when its relevance came to an end.

16. Mike

So my connection with Mike was evidently next on the agenda. My connection to Sally was inspiring, but apparently there was a fair amount of importance attached to my relationship to Mike, as well. A vague memory of being in trenches with him came and went, then came again, but it was unsharp as an image or memory, more like a bookmark than a book. Behind it I saw many other lives, even one suggesting I had been married to him! I was his wife, apparently. It didn't feel too important, just slightly relevant. But I was unable to concentrate on it or make any meaningful interpretations.

Then I was back in his Portslade workshop where he was apparently dismantling a machine of sorts. I realised it was Sound World, the machine he'd made as a student. It was partly in pieces yet still recognisable. He had pulleys, bicycle chains and gears with him and all manner of other bits and pieces. And my drum set. He was taking everything apart.

I laughed so loud (yet soundlessly) when I realised what he was up to, he stopped in his tracks and looked around the empty workshop for someone to appear. I mean, this had been a strange trip for all of us and Mike had never been spiritually aware - like any of us in fact. But I had been quite amused by his ease of accepting my strange presence from early on, without questioning or altering his own beliefs or standpoint. Now he was rebuilding his student project as a kind of otherworldly drum machine. My first thought was about the delay that would no doubt happen. My iPad impulse would become a mechanical impulse that would take time to reach the skins. While I thought about that problem, I also came up with a possible solution. As it was within my grasp to manipulate time, there might be a way of keeping the beat a short time ahead, say one fifth of a second, to allow for the time it would take for the bass drum pedal to reach the bass drum, for example. At least the bass drum pedal system offered the mechanics he needed to get started and with electric motors and some clever electronic switching, it would be the easiest and I could see this is what gave Mike the idea to begin with. But how to get the app to export each individual item accurately? The hi-hat and the cymbals, though visually quite similar, used a completely different technique to export their sound. I could see that was puzzling him and he was working on combining with an electronic drum set, which looked like a ready-made option to me. But despite all his knowledge of digital subject matter, he was in his heart of hearts an analogue man and loved the world of mechanical, physical instruments.

Having said that, he got up to sit in one of his prized office chairs and dragged his feet to the desktop computer, which he booted up and opened to pages of code. This was, and frankly still is, beyond me, but at least it gave me access to a keyboard and thus two-way communication.

I wrote,

"Hey Mike, giving the Sound World a new lease of life?"

"Wow, Geoff, don't startle me like that! Glad to see you're still around though. Yes, well if I get this right, we can perform live with you again, or use the recordings. I'm trying to make sure both versions work."

"Surprised you still have all that gear. Must be about 25 years old now!"

"Probably. But I've often cannibalised it for various other projects. Still got most of the original tapes and sensors. May put a more modern version of it together if this doesn't work."

I typed:

"Why shouldn't it work? Looks promising to me."

"Glad you think so, Geoff. Not quite sure how to fix the mechanical delay that's sure to happen."

"I've been thinking about that as well. If I'm in this in-between state, I reckon I can alter my perceived time and get the timing right."

Mike turned on his office chair and looked exactly in my direction. So strange that he couldn't see me, I wondered how he could be aware of exactly where I was. His face was full of enthusiasm, I felt a really strong connection to him at that moment.

"You think that would work? Hey, not all parts are working but maybe we can try out the bass drum to begin with. It's actually already good to go."

My bass drum actually had two pedals so was ready-made for enhancement. I had a close (actually very close) look at what he'd been up to. Mike had added two micro-switches and a pair of rapidly responsive electro motors. There was a bit of play in all the connections, which was a good thing, allowing for some delay through reverberation. He could have done much of this more easily with a drum machine, but I understood the need for live character. Next he was bending over his iPad and typed,

"I can't find a simple way of connecting the hi-hat, crash and ride cymbals, china cymbals, tom and snare, so I may have to fall back on a drum machine, which would be a pity, but at least the bass drum would still be authentic."

The bass drum was a very important part of our whole group and the double nature of the pedals ensured a rapid speed up wherever necessary. Which was quite frequently. But some of the most unusual stuff we used, particularly for Death Metal, was with brushes on introductions. We used them quite a lot and they were something of a trademark. I watched Mike working at his contraption, looking sometimes quite excited when he thought something might work out. He would smile from time to time, sharing the moments with me, almost always looking in the right direction, too. It was a challenge to connect the brushes and sticks as they need to be flexible and accurate and I believe he was occasionally having doubts about the whole exercise. It was a long way from being a robot, but it did have potential. The default was the drum app and speakers, so Mike had the security of our last gig, with added, more complicated trimmings. He continued working out some weird connections and to hear a real crash of cymbals or beat on a snare did make a difference, however large and powerful the fall-back speakers were.

So we had a go, and the thump, thump, thump of the bass drum, a real bass drum, made an enormous difference. Next we tried the tom-tom and snare drum which worked with slightly less pressure than I would have used but he was getting there and I was caught up in his excitement too. The brackets and angles he had to put together were well thought out, but I didn't know how well they'd survive a 2-hour gig. I could see he was pleased, but I also saw doubt in his expression as he opened the chat programme after a couple of minutes.

"Thing is, how long are you going to be around Geoff? I mean we will need to think about replacing you at some point, won't we?"

"I'm pretty sure it won't be for ever, Mike. What do you suggest, to go along with it for the next gig and see how it works?"

"Yeah, I can't really see past the next gig. Taking one at a time seems like an idea. Haywards Heath was spectacular, but it may have been a one off. We have a Brighton gig next week, should we give it a spin?"

Although it seemed a bit odd for me to be in on the decision making, as an idea it sounded reasonable, and I suggested he asked Patrick and Jay to be sure.

....

So, 'Vallhalla Victims' agreed and we were good to go. Patrick was still a bit concerned about his dad's attitude to the whole thing, but Jay thought as long as they didn't have a replacement for me it would be a cool way to play and might even give us an added mystery, with the moniker of being the smallest 4-piece band in the world. We had two rehearsals before the next gig and they worked out like a dream. In fact, it was just like old times, except I wasn't really there.

17. Brighton

We had a different kind of following in Brighton to elsewhere in Sussex or other counties or countries we played in. They were critical and appreciative at the same time, but with the understanding that we wouldn't be where we were, if it hadn't been for their early wisdom in recognising our potential. A kind of snobbish, yet honest appraisal of the group as an entity which in some ways belonged to its original fans, who knew and had listened to our early work with fierce loyalty once we had passed the test of authenticity, which they alone were in a position to judge. They also were a mixed bunch, some new fans from this millennium, who had picked up on our recent popularity as well as followers who claimed had helped us to 'stardom' in the 90s.

I saw the guys were approaching the gig with some trepidation, not only because of the idiosyncrasy of our fans, but also the first public outing with Mike's drumming contraption. I said I'd be there in spirit, a concept now none of them had a problem with, but I was going to play along the way I previously had in Hayward's Heath, but with a built-in catch-up in the drumbeat. It had worked well at rehearsals, but we all knew there was a risk involved. As a band whose strength had always been live music, we didn't want to alienate our fans with too much electronic manipulation.

Jack was scared to put the drum set together, so he left it to Mike.

"I'm not touching that, Mike, it looks like it might go off!"

He was right, it did look a bit like an improvised explosive device of some sort, but Mike was confident it would work.

"Well you'd remember how explosive Geoff's drumming was!"

A general groan followed that comment but the band members within listening distance were all looking forward to the gig. Jack didn't understand why Mike had gone to all this trouble, but Jay and Patrick were in on our secret and to them it made perfect sense. As far as Jack was concerned, he was still using the recordings I had made before the accident.

The location was a pub near the Bear Road in Brighton, that had just opened its own concert room. Mainly aimed at jazz bands, it was a reasonable size for a first gig and had access to the rear end of the bar, so people were going to have to put up with a certain amount of added volume if they were sitting in the pub itself. They served craft beer and their own massive casks made up part of the decor in the concert room. It would hold less than 100 people we had been told, and Jay negotiated low ticket prices in recognition of our gratitude to the Brighton public. They weren't exactly hand-picked, but we had been careful to limit publicity to avoid disappointment if people found they couldn't get in.

Mary arrived for the sound check and came with a guy who looked vaguely familiar. He was quite tall, had a reddish tinge in his beard, but I couldn't place him for the moment. There are ways of doing this when you are on the other side, but the law of non-interference is so strong that most would steer clear of invading someone's privacy. The place soon began to fill up, so I lost sight of him and everyone else, apart from a few familiar faces who'd been with us for years and never seemed to tire of our repertoire.

Patrick started off growling the intro to 'The Gates of Valhalla' on his own, which was often a good way to warm up. The brushes were working well, and then I changed to the sticks and bass when the music began and it seemed to be just like in the old days with the diehard enthusiasts up front, singing or growling along with their version of our lyrics. I felt we were a bit close to the public, the 'stage' was less than a foot high, there was space between us and the bar, where people could order drinks, despite the noise. As a result, as drummer, I was much closer than usual to the public.

Although aware of the shapes and forms our music was generating, I didn't focus on them as I had done in Hayward's Heath. My concentration was on getting the timing right - always a drummer's main job - but allowing for the delay built in to the mechanics of Mike's machine. Different items needed different delays, so I was witnessing rather bizarre packets of the future in small portions of reality. It hadn't been this hard at our practice sessions, but the live atmosphere made it more of a challenge with additional ambient noise to combat. About halfway through our first half I felt something was going to change, an event, for want of a better word, had announced itself in one of these small packets of the future.

There was a slightly drunk guy behind the stage who had just gone to order another beer, when his return was hampered by the low stage we were using and he tripped, taking his pint of bitter with him, which splashed over the iPad and into some of the electric and electronic connections that Mike had so meticulously built. I felt sorry for him immediately, he wasn't that worse for wear because of alcohol consumption, but the height of the stage, such as it was, had been so low that he missed it completely on his way back to his mates, just across my corner of the stage.

He had a slight cut on his brow that was bleeding a little, probably from bumping into a cymbal, but his apologies were so profuse, the band gathered round him to see if all was well. Accidents can happen, although I had seen it somewhat differently. It wasn't an accident, it was something that was 'supposed' to happen. Something that would bring about change. Change was imperative for the band, that was a certainty for me at that moment.

Mary and Jay fussed over him with some first aid, yet he seemed more embarrassed than hurt. The atmosphere had just been warming up to that temperature we all looked forward to, no matter what or where the gig was taking place. Whether in Wacken or a tiny pub in Brighton, there was a certain level where the crowd would pick up on our volume and speed and frontman Patrick would have them in his hand to mould and care for in his own inimitable style.

This moment had come and gone and the room's apparent temperature had dropped back to normal. I felt a crisis in Mike's life and turned my attention to him. Patrick was apologising for the 'technical difficulties' and asked the audience to bear with us while we got back on track.

Beer moisture had apparently ruined Mike's connections, maybe even short circuited some of them. I saw him desperately try and dry out the iPad, but he seemed to be aware it would be a hopeless effort while the band was hoping to perform again within a few moments. He looked at Patrick.

"What do you think, should we ask him?"

"Who?" Patrick asked with a desperate look in his eyes. "Oh, you mean Marc? Yeah, let's do that. Geoff deserves a night off anyway."

I always enjoyed Patrick's humour and this was no exception. I watched and listened as they brought the break forward by a few minutes and he told the audience we would be back soon. His gag about being the smallest 4 piece band in the world was coming to an end.

Mary had left the guy with his minor injury by this time where I saw her approaching the young guy she had come in with. This was Marc, apparently. I saw him scratch his beard and shrug his shoulders and followed her to the stage, where Mike was already putting together a standard drum kit by separating out the parts he needed while Jack brought some replacement gear in from the van.

Suddenly I remembered where I had last seen Marc and it came to me in a complete explanation. This was the young man I had seen at the back of the church with his mother, Geraldine. Mike's nephew. My son. Oh my god, he was my son.

I felt a rush through my whole being at that moment and a realisation. Much as I wanted to approach him and love him after well over 20 years as an absent father, I had another spontaneous insight.

Blurry images of Marc and me from another life were flooding into my consciousness. Pillaging came to mind. We were knights in armour and although the armour may have been shining we had left our wives and children at home alone for years, while the rush we got from rape and pillage kept us on a high for many years. Ironically, I saw that we had been Norsemen. We had lived in a place that looked somewhat like Ireland to me, where we had other wives and even kept slaves. We had been brutal and powerful and had supported each other through our worst episodes of scaring and destroying whole communities.

I was shown only a brief glimpse of my biological son in this life, or rather, after it, and it took me away from the current scene in the pub with immediate effect. But I understood and remembered quite a number of facts in my life. If you have been an absent father, you need to have one yourself at some time. And Marc apparently needed me as his absent father to complete his circle. The irony wasn't lost on me that we had a Scandinavian connection and in this role he was replacing me. He actually still had a Scandinavian look, which I had obviously lost, but the combination of Geraldine's genes and mine would have ensured a suitable DNA soup to provide him with the appropriate appearance.

We were only Valhalla Victims, but the names Jason and John Bonham came to mind. No doubt there have been other replacements in a father and son drumming role, but to be vaguely connected this way to Led Zeppelin felt like a real honour. As far as I could tell, his drumming skills made him well prepared for the Victims' music.

Meanwhile, I felt John's presence approaching, enveloping me in a different environment.

18.Jay and Marc

John took me to a kind of library, which might be described as the study area for past, present and future lives and learning. I should have remembered it from my last visit, from previous lives, which were all stored there and available for review whenever needed.

He looked at me with wisdom and respect.

"Your connection to Marc was important in the context of your last life, but the absent fatherhood has now been fulfilled. Do you remember where it began?"

"Well it was a life that I vaguely remember, but tell me more." He gave me a 'Don't give me that crap' look and I had to laugh. Despite my reaction a screen came out of the floor and three dimensional scenes began unfolding before my eyes. They seemed life-size too, which meant it was emotionally uncomfortably close for re-experiencing past events.

I recognised Bo, (Marc in this life) and my name was Arne. It was our life as Vikings in Ireland that I had felt when I had seen Marc join the band in the pub. Riding horses and wearing protective armour, we were well equipped with swords and daggers. We had come to destroy a village that had not being supplying us with the fresh meat and grain as agreed. We had agreed to this, but the village hadn't, a fact that didn't stop us from considering it an agreement. In fact, it was quite a small settlement, but Bo and I were intoxicated by the feeling of power it gave us, to destroy a group of people just because we could, our rivalry pushing us to outdo each other in brutality. The villagers who managed to escape were of no interest, but those left behind would be killed.

I wanted to look away as I now knew where this was going, but the scene just followed my consciousness, wherever it tried to focus. A small fire in the middle of the settlement, used by the population as a constant source for their needs, was where we were heading and Bo overturned its framework with a smart kick of his boot, and following his lead, I picked up a burning branch and set alight to the roofs of their small dwellings, while he did the same on the other side. People came screaming out of their homes and with a blow of our swords, we finished them off as quickly as we could.

I wanted John to stop this story unfolding, but with his customary humour, he said,

"You were right bastards, weren't you? But wait, the best is yet to come."

That comment took the edge off my fears, because he doesn't truly judge a life. That is apparently up to each individual and he was mirroring the thoughts which were in my mind while I was watching this horror before me. It was a dreadful, frightening scene to watch. My latest life had only just ended but the rawness and contrast to what I was viewing couldn't have been greater. I even felt the thrill it gave us both to carry out such abominations, which was a hard emotion to relive. The settlement was now lost, to all intents and purposes. All their modest buildings were burning, the population of probably only 30 or 40 people dead or escaped and we felt triumph in our cowardice. We began to make our way back to our home, commenting to each other that 'it would teach them a lesson'. This felt hollow and meaningless now in my between-life state, but it was a sentiment I had then truly believed.

We lived on top of the next hill, and Bo rushed off to arrive first at our dwelling, always keen to compete. I was taking it slowly up a steep path, my horse unwilling to be rushed.

I noticed movement in the bushes ahead and a small person came out and stood a few yards ahead in my path. It was a girl of maybe 10 or 11 and with one blow of my sword she would have joined the others, but I was halted by her expression of helplessness combined with fearlessness. Perhaps she was aware of her fate and just wanted it to be over and done with, but her expression was too strong to look away and I was drawn to her green eyes and decided to speak with her.

"Out of my way, little girl." She didn't move but continued to look self possessed and defiant.

"It's up to you sir. Either kill me now or take me home with you and look after me."

She had no fear of death, that was obvious, but even I couldn't bring myself to a cold-blooded slaughter.

"I can milk cows and sheep. I know how to make butter. I know how to take care of crops. I make bread. I tend chicken too and use their eggs in cooking. I can make myself useful if you look after me."

I bent down without another word and hauled her up to share the saddle with me. She didn't seem particularly grateful or even surprised.

The thought came to me that it was the first time I had shown kindness in this life. The wind must have blown moisture into my eyes as I found I had to wipe them to see clearly where we were going.

"Well, it wasn't the only time you were kind, but the moments were quite rare," John smiled as the scene faded. He didn't need to tell me who this little girl had been, as I knew already it was my 'half-brother' Jay, with whom I almost shared a name. I almost shared a family with him too and we shared a taste in music which had brought us to where we now happened to be.

19.Saying Goodbye

It was time to go and take my leave of friends and family. I managed to surprise Patrick, who was just sending a text message to Mary.

"Hey Patrick, I'm finally leaving. Marc is a good replacement, it's all good. Love you man, and see you!"

He replied with a couple of crying emojis. I found one which was looking friendly and joyful and entered the same number of images. His hand covered his mouth, I could tell he was suppressing emotions, as he said out loud,

"See you Geoff. It's been great. Like nothing on Earth."

With that he closed his smartphone case and slumped onto his swivel chair with a sigh.

....

Mike I found at the workshop. Not surprisingly, he was dismantling 'our' drum set.

"Mike," I wrote on his desktop. "Just called to say goodbye."

"Oh, right. So it's all over?"

"Pretty much. But it was a fun experience."

"Well, yeah," he wrote back. "But it might have been more fun if you'd managed to stay alive!"

"Are you sure about that?" He was considering the implications of that last statement and I saw him shrug.

"Well, we did experience some extraordinary stuff, that's true."

"Just leave me an old laptop or something on standby, ok?" He looked puzzled, but interested.

"Sure. Now you've got my attention. Why?"

"You'll see. Look out for a file called 'Life after', ok?"

"Will do. So you're not disappearing completely?" I wasn't quite sure how to answer that, but it felt as if my life was complete, even though I still had some writing to do.

"Don't think so. But life is over now. I won't interfere with yours anymore."

"Hey, let's high-five. Would be a great way to say goodbye!" So we did and the connection felt like 220 volts. He grinned in my direction and settled back to his work, with the devotion that defined him.

....

Jay was on the phone to a client when I found him.

"So we will use 90% of the remaining budget for online ads. The rest will be just in case we need some posters or other print media. Are we agreed on that?" Apparently the client was in agreement, and he brought the conversation to a close soon after that. He was standing at a lectern with his laptop open, and I looked for an open programme.

The keyboard reacted quickly to my message.

"Jay. I need to take my leave."

"Geoff," he wrote, "don't go. Oh, boy. Don't go yet, anyway. I had this weird dream I wanted to tell you about. Just last night." It was almost as if he'd been expecting me.

"Okay. What did you want to tell me?"

"I had this dream that was so real, I need to let you know."

Apparently Jay had dreamed of being a fearless little girl who saw some goodness in a brutal Viking who had just destroyed the village she had lived in. Appealing to his better nature, she persuaded him to take her with him. Although many years older than her, Arne, this Viking guy, who looked just like me, had taken good care of her and later they had a family together and Arne's friend Bo looked just like the band's new drummer, Marc.

"Wow. Well I knew some bits of that, too. Didn't know we'd had a family, though!"

"What!? You think this was all true? It certainly seemed very real. A previous life or what?"

"Yes, it looks like it. I became aware of it myself in the in-between state."

"Sounds so crazy. Better not tell anyone, I might get certified!"

"You might indeed," I replied with a series of emojis crying with laughter.

"There are more things in heaven and earth, Horatio, than are dreamt of in your philosophy," he quoted. Hamlet. The only other Shakespeare play we had studied together at school.

"And the whole world's a stage," I replied. It was an obvious reply, and he gave me the only possible response.

"I'll let you be in my dreams if I can be in yours!"

"I said that." Jay closed his laptop and with his hands on his neck went to the window, as if able to see me departing.

Perhaps he could.

Saying goodbye to Sally was going to the easiest and the hardest at the same time.

Easiest because I could reach her dreams with ease, but hardest because our connection was the strongest of all, and I didn't want to lose it or its reminder of a physical body. The body has limits whereas the spirit appears to have none, but the very limits of the body are what make it such an important, irreplaceable piece of personal history.

Sally was on her own most of the time now, if she wasn't working. She was self-sufficient as far as she could be, eating much of the produce from her own garden and able to be on her own for long, without missing anyone in particular. She was an active lucid dreamer, though I don't know how much her daily mind was aware of where she went in her dreams. But a rerun of our previous meeting in our garden would be a perfect way to say our goodbyes.

Sally wouldn't be Sally if she wasn't the one in control, and when I went looking for her in the garden, in the gloom of the night, she was nowhere to be seen. An irresistible suction movement took me to the beach below the cliffs of Birling Gap. Where I saw her dancing and floating on and above the beach. It almost looked like a ritual of some kind, but was, as it happens, much more down to earth.

"Dance with me, Geoff! Come and dance with me!" Despite having a good grip on rhythm and timing as a drummer, my attempts at dancing on the Earth were always pretty dreadful. Sally loved dancing, yet she would dance with a girlfriend, rather than suffer the embarrassment of dancing with me and my awkward moves. This time it was different.

I reached up to hold her hand and she led me to dance with skill and - dare I say it? - beauty that I had never before experienced. Like collections of cosmic dust in human form we danced over the beach, where she showed me the exact spot where my mortal remains had been disbursed as dust by the Victims.

"I don't know how you did it, but you formed the shape of a bass drum, before dissipating into the atmosphere."

"Sally, that wasn't me. I have no memory or idea what that you are describing."

"Consciousness is everywhere, I suppose," as she drew me over the cliff top to stand on the earth again and admire the view in this twilight, pulsating version of Birling Gap, as I had never seen it before.

"Maybe it was one of John's little jokes? I suggested.

"I wouldn't put it past him!" Laughing at the idea, we started to dance again, a really close and slow blues, cheek to cosmic cheek. The music was in our heads.

"I have to go soon, my love. You do know that?"

"Of course. This is our 'Last Waltz', right?"

"Yes, but I'm more skilled at it now than when I was still alive!" Sally laughed at that.

"You can say that again!" Streams of sparks filled the air around us as her laughter filled the area with joy. In my life, I might have been offended at being laughed at, but in this state, I recognised her joy as being the perfect expression for a set of rules which we played out and kept to, during our lives together. There was even a reason for my inability to dance on Earth, although I wasn't too bothered about knowing why. Just knowing there are reasons behind things was a thought strong enough to feel inspired by it all.

At that moment, I realised what Sally was up to. We were joined by John - she was handing me over to him!

"Wait! No, don't go!" We embraced in a melding of our energies and a sparkling stream of love surrounded us, evidently added to by John.

In one of John's frequent excursions into modern life and humour, Arnold Schwarzenegger's Terminator face briefly replaced his own.

"Hasta la Vista, baby!" Sally's smiling face was so close that it filled my field of vision.

"I'll let you be in my dreams if I can be in yours!" Sally said that and I watched as her form receded into the distance. John and I stayed for a moment, standing next to each other in respect towards Sally. There was no hiding the admiration we felt and the love she gave to those who knew her as well as complete strangers who happened to cross her path.

....

20.Epilogue

Hi Mike,

this is a manuscript I have written about our experiences, mainly covering the time after my accident with the van. You and the guys are a very important part of it, of course. You can do what you like with it, but two things I would like to ask you are:

1). Keep the title: Valhalla Victims, Life after Death Metal

2). If you can't get a publisher, put it online. There are plenty of places for online publishing for amateurs like myself. In fact, that might be the better choice in any case.

I hope Marc is a successful replacement for me. I'm sure he'll do well. Give my love to everyone.

Cheers, mate.

Geoff

Copyright

Quoted copyright information:

The Night They Drove Old Dixie Down

Written by © Robbie Robertson (the Band)

Canaan Music Inc

The Boxer

(Just a come on from the whores on 7th Avenue)

Written and published by © Paul Simon

When a man loves a woman

Written by © Calvin Lewis, Andrew Wright

Published by SGAE

Two Silhouettes

(Took a walk and passed your house late last night

All the shades were pulled and drawn way down tight)

Written by: © Bob Crewe, Frank C. Slay, Frank Slay Jr

Regent Music Corporation, Regent Music

Here comes the Sun

Written by © George Harrison, Harrisongs

Into the Mystic

Written by © Van Morrison

Caledonia Soulmusic MusicWarner Bros Inc

Full Metal Village

Documentary film © Cho Sung-hyung

Bye bye love

(Bye bye sweet caress, hello emptiness, I feel like I could die.')

Written by © Felice and Boudleaux Bryant

Universal Music Publishing Group

The Big Lebowski

Crime Comedy Film 1998, © Ethan and Joel Coen

Unforgettable with Natalie and Nat King Cole

Written by © Irving Gordon

Bourne Co Music Publishers

Unchained Melody

Written by © Alex North and lyrics by Hy Zaret

Unchained Melody Publishing LLC

Ghost

Romantic fantasy thriller 1990

Directed by © Jerry Zucker

Talking World War III Blues

(I'll let you be in my dreams if I can be in yours)

Written by © Bob Dylan 1963

Terminator 2: Judgment Day

(Hasta la vista, baby)

Science fiction film directed by © James Cameron 1991

Herstellung und Verlag:
BoD – Books on Demand, Norderstedt
ISBN:978-3-7494-7993-1

FSC

www.fsc.org

MIX

Papier aus ver-
antwortungsvollen
Quellen
Paper from
responsible sources

FSC® C105338